My Treasury of
PRINCESS
Tales

hinkler

This book belongs to

Matteud...........

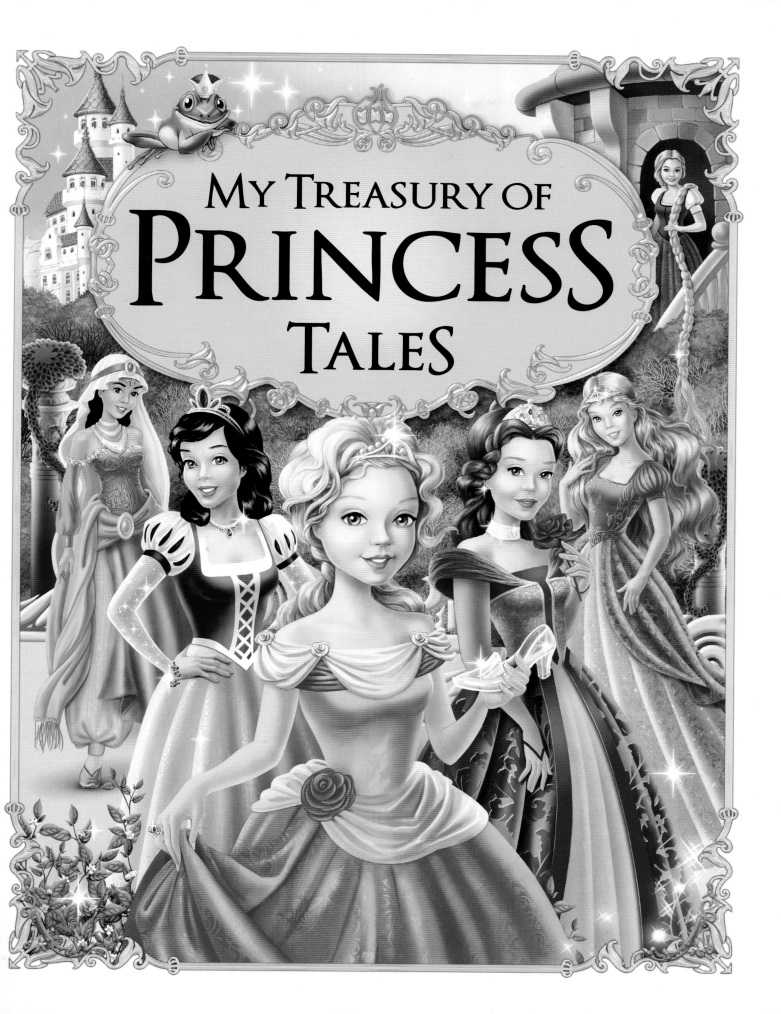

My Treasury of
PRINCESS
TALES

Published by Hinkler Books Pty Ltd
45–55 Fairchild Street
Heatherton Victoria 3202 Australia
www.hinkler.com.au

hinkler

© Hinkler Books Pty Ltd 2012

Editor: Louise Coulthard
Art director: Paul Scott
Cover illustrator: Mirela Tufan
Illustrators: Melissa Webb, Suzie Byrne, Mirela Tufan, Dean Jones and Brijbasi Art Press
Prepress: Graphic Print Group

ISBN 978 1 7430 8000 9

Printed and bound in China

Contents

Introduction

Every little girl dreams of being a fairytale princess. Nothing quite captures the imagination like the magical world of royalty, make-believe and romance. Princesses of traditional fairytales live in glorious, glistening palaces, dance at magical balls wearing beautiful gowns spun from pure gold, ride in enchanted carriages pulled by magnificent horses and, of course, fall in love with handsome princes!

The princesses of these stories are classic fairytale heroines that come from a range of different folktale traditions. These include the scholarly collections of the Brothers Grimm of 18th- and 19th-century Germany, the imaginative stories of Hans Christian Andersen of 19th-century Denmark and the courtly tales of Charles Perrault of 17th-century France.

It is a testament to these stories' incredible longevity that they resonate as strongly with young readers of today as they did with those of over a hundred years ago. Share and retell these tales with your little girls and you'll be joining the rich tradition of parents and children enjoying a special, magical time together.

Every little girl wants to feel as special as a princess. Use these tales to help reinforce the message that each little girl is unique and extraordinary: a princess in her own right.

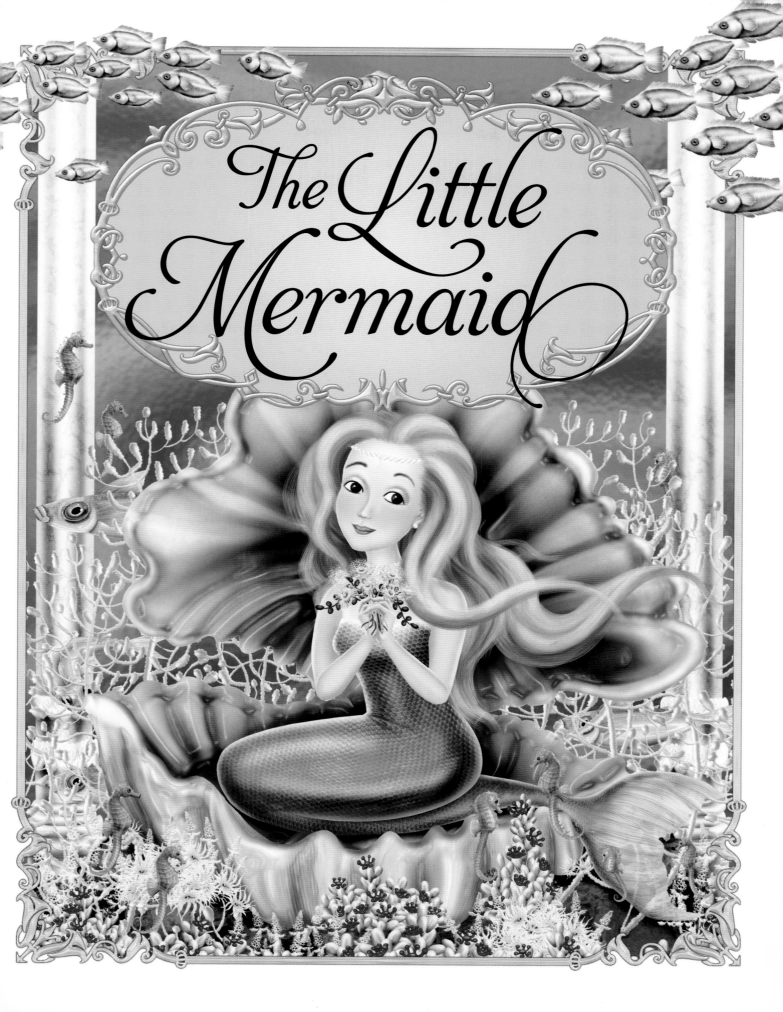

The Little Mermaid

Far out in the deep ocean, where the water is as blue as the sky and as clear as crystal, there lived the Sea King and his six daughters. He lived in a beautiful castle with walls made of coral, windows of amber and a roof of shells that opened and closed as the water flowed over them. Inside each shell was a glittering pearl. The castle was surrounded by a garden of lovely, colourful sea plants and flowers and was filled with fish both large and small.

The Sea King's wife had died many years ago, so his aging mother kept house for him. She was very old and wise and looked after the sea princesses. The Sea King's youngest daughter was the most beautiful of all, with skin as delicate as a rose petal and eyes as blue as the sea. Like all sea people, she had no legs and her body ended in a fish's tail.

All day the princesses played in the halls of the castle or swam in the gardens. Each of the princesses had their own little garden in the castle grounds where they could dig and plant whatever they wished. One had a flower bed in the shape of a whale, another made her's like a shell, but the youngest princess's garden was shaped like the sun, which could be seen in calm weather, shining down like a great flower. Her garden was full of red and yellow flowers, like the rays of the sun at dusk.

The only thing the youngest princess cared for more than her pretty flowers was a beautiful marble statue of a handsome boy. It was carved out of pure white stone and had fallen to the bottom of the sea from a wrecked ship. She loved to hear stories of the world above the sea. Her grandmother would tell her about ships, towns, people and animals.

'When you have turned fifteen,' said her grandmother, 'you will be allowed to swim to the surface, to sit on the rocks and see the great ships, the forests and the towns.'

When the oldest sister turned fifteen, she swam to the surface to see the world above. When she returned, she told her younger sisters such wonderful tales. She told them of the moonlight on a sandbank, the twinkling lights of a town, the sound of music and voices and the ringing of the church bells. The youngest sister longed to see these wonderful things.

As the years passed, each sister turned fifteen, and was allowed to swim to the surface to see the world above. The second sister returned with tales of the sunset, the sky golden with red clouds scurrying across it and a flock of wild swans flying towards the sun.

The third sister was the bravest and swam up a wide river. She saw green hills, palaces and castles, forests and birds. She came across little children playing in the river and wanted to join them, but a little black animal came and barked at her so she swam away. It was a dog but she had never seen one before.

The fourth sister stayed in the ocean, but saw great ships as large as castles, their sails white in the sun. She swam with leaping dolphins and saw huge whales spurting water into the air.

The fifth sister's birthday was in the winter. When she swam to the surface, she saw enormous icebergs, like huge, glittering pearls. She sat on an iceberg and watched a storm, with dark clouds, rolling thunder and blue lightning, darting across the sky.

Once they had turned fifteen, the older sisters could swim to the surface whenever they wished. But after a few months, they decided they preferred to stay at home. However, in the evenings, the five older sisters would swim together to the surface and sing to the sailors on the ships about the delights of the ocean, but the sailors never understood, thinking it was just the wind.

Finally, the youngest sister turned fifteen. She bade farewell to her grandmother and swam to the surface. The sun was just setting as she raised her head above the waves and the sky was crimson and gold. A large ship with three masts sat in the water. It was stuck where it sat, for there was no breeze at all, and the sailors were making merry on the deck. Music was playing and the ship was lit up with lanterns.

The mermaid swam closer to the ship and looked in the cabin windows. She saw a number of finely dressed people inside. Among them was a handsome young prince. It was his sixteenth birthday and everyone on the ship was celebrating.

The young prince went up to the deck, and suddenly hundreds of rockets rose into the air. The little mermaid was amazed as she watched the fireworks exploding and falling like stars. How handsome the prince looked as he watched the fireworks!

As time passed, the sailors put out the lanterns, but still the little mermaid watched. The sea started to become restless and the waves grew higher. As the wind rose, the sailors unfurled the sails and the ship continued on its way, but still the mermaid followed. Soon dark clouds were racing across the sky and a terrible storm approached. The waves rose higher and higher.

Soon, the main mast groaned and then snapped off. Some of the planks of the ship came loose. The little mermaid could see the sailors holding on with all their might, but she could not see the handsome prince.

Suddenly, a flash of lightning crashed across the sky and the little mermaid saw him struggling in the water. As the prince sank down, she swam to him. His eyes were closed and he was not moving. She helped him to the surface and kept his head above the water until morning.

As the sun rose and the storm passed, there was no sign of the ship. They were in sight of land and so the little mermaid took the prince in to shore. There were green hills in the distance and a large white building like a church or a convent. The little mermaid laid the unconscious prince in the sand.

Then a bell rang in the distance and some young girls came out of the white building. The little mermaid swam out to sea and hid behind some rocks. One young girl walked to the beach, where she found the prince lying in the sand. The prince came to and smiled at the girl, and then many people came to help him. But the prince had no smile for the little mermaid, as he did not know she had rescued him. The little mermaid was very unhappy as the prince was led away into the white building. She returned home to the Sea King's castle.

After this, the little mermaid was always quiet and sad. She often swam to the beach where she had left the prince, but she never saw him. Her only comfort was to sit in her garden, but she let the flowers grow wild and it became very dark and gloomy.

At last she asked her sisters and they showed her where the prince's palace was. The little mermaid spent many days and nights in the sea near the palace, watching him. She saw him sailing his boat or walking on the shore. As she watched, she also saw other people and heard fisherman talking. She grew more and more fond of humans. Finally, she went to her grandmother and asked, 'Do humans live forever?'

'No,' replied her grandmother. 'They must die, and they do not live as long as we do. But when we die, we become the foam on the surface of the ocean and have no immortal souls. Humans have a soul that lives forever, even after they die.'

'So I will die and never hear the music of the waves or see the red sun. Is there nothing I can do to gain an immortal soul?' asked the little mermaid.

'Only if a man were to love you so much that you meant everything to him and he promised to be true to you alone,' replied her grandmother. 'But this could never happen, for we cannot walk among them. Be happy and swim in the ocean.'

The little mermaid was not content. She decided to visit the Sea Witch. She travelled past foaming whirlpools and bubbling mud. The Sea Witch's house lay in the middle of a strange forest full of plants with slimy branches like worms. The witch's house was made of bones and was surrounded by fat water snakes.

'I know what you want,' the Sea Witch said when she saw the little mermaid. 'You are very silly. You will get what you wish, but it will bring you nothing but sadness. You want legs like a human so the prince will fall in love with you and give you an immortal soul.'

The little mermaid nodded. The Sea Witch laughed and said, 'I will make you a potion. Swim to the shore before sunrise and drink it. Your tail will be replaced by legs, but every step will feel like you are standing on sharp knives. You can never be a mermaid again nor return to your home and family. And if the prince does not love you and marries another, you will become the foam on the waves. If you can bear that, I will help you.'

'I can bear it,' said the little mermaid.

'I must be paid,' said the Sea Witch. 'You have the sweetest voice of all the creatures of the sea. You must give it to me.'

The little mermaid was sad but she agreed. The witch prepared the potion and took the little mermaid's voice. The little mermaid returned home, where everyone was asleep. She took a flower from each of her sisters' gardens to remember them, and then swam away for the last time. She swam to shore and drank the potion, then swooned. The next thing she knew, the sun was up and the handsome prince was standing before her.

She realised that instead of her fish tail, she had legs. The prince asked where she was from but she could not answer, as she had no voice. The prince took her back to his castle. Every step felt as though she was walking on needles, but she walked gracefully. They dressed her in robes of silk and she was the most beautiful woman in the palace, but she could not speak.

The prince was charmed by her beauty and said she should stay with him always. She accompanied him everywhere he went. As the days passed, she loved the prince more and more, and he loved her as he would love a child, but he never thought to marry her.

'You are dear to me,' the prince told her, 'but there is only one woman in the world I could love. I was shipwrecked and the waves cast me to shore near a church. A young woman found me there and saved my life. She serves the church still.'

'He doesn't know it was me who saved him,' thought the little mermaid. 'I was the one who carried him to shore and I saw the pretty maid he loves more than me. But he shan't marry her as she serves the church.'

It was decided by the king and queen that the prince should marry. The daughter of a nearby king was to be his wife, so the little mermaid went on a ship with the prince and his court to visit them.

'I must visit her,' said the prince to the little mermaid, 'but they cannot force me to love her or marry her.'

One night as the ship was sailing, the little mermaid sat on the deck looking at the waves. She thought she could see her father's castle in the waters below. Then her sisters came to the surface and waved to her. She beckoned to them, but a cabin boy came by and so they dived down.

The next morning, the ship sailed into the beautiful harbour of the king. There was a big parade waiting to meet them. The princess had not yet arrived, as she was being educated in a church to learn the royal virtues.

At last she arrived and the little mermaid had to admit she was the most beautiful woman she'd ever seen. She was fair, with laughing blue eyes that shone with truth and purity.

When he saw her, the prince let out a cry and exclaimed, 'It was you who saved me when I lay shipwrecked on the beach! Oh, I am too happy! All my dreams have come true.'

He took the princess in his arms. The little mermaid felt as though her heart was breaking. She knew that when he married, she would change into the foam of the waves by the next morning and would never have an immortal soul.

That night, the prince was married, but the little mermaid only thought of the death that was coming to her. She was dressed in beautiful silks and she danced more gracefully than she had ever danced before. Even though it hurt her tender feet, she did not feel it, because the pain in her heart was much greater. The prince took his bride to his ship where the celebrations continued into the night. Then the ship grew quiet as everyone fell asleep.

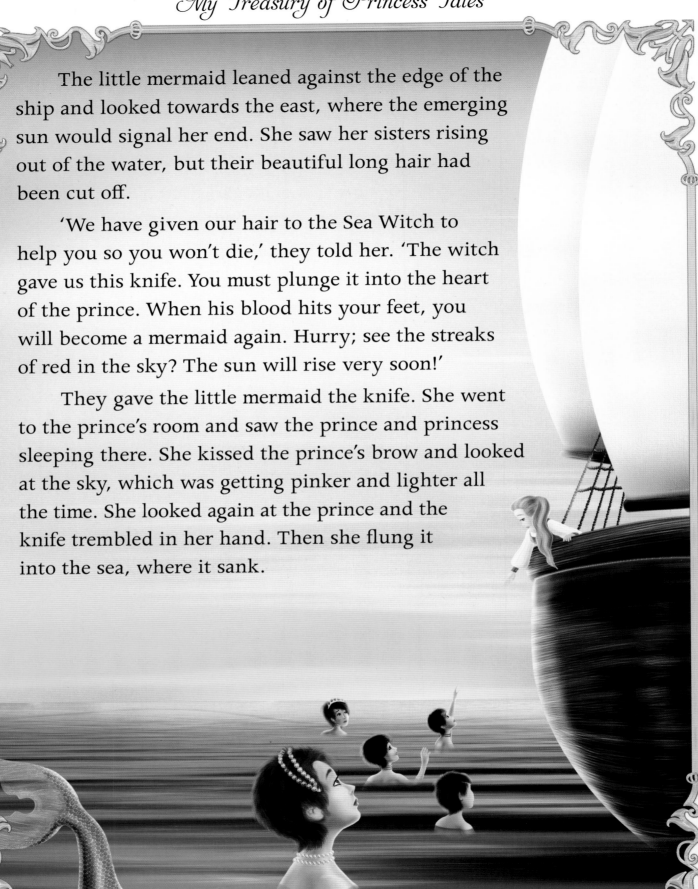

The little mermaid leaned against the edge of the ship and looked towards the east, where the emerging sun would signal her end. She saw her sisters rising out of the water, but their beautiful long hair had been cut off.

'We have given our hair to the Sea Witch to help you so you won't die,' they told her. 'The witch gave us this knife. You must plunge it into the heart of the prince. When his blood hits your feet, you will become a mermaid again. Hurry; see the streaks of red in the sky? The sun will rise very soon!'

They gave the little mermaid the knife. She went to the prince's room and saw the prince and princess sleeping there. She kissed the prince's brow and looked at the sky, which was getting pinker and lighter all the time. She looked again at the prince and the knife trembled in her hand. Then she flung it into the sea, where it sank.

The little mermaid threw herself into the sea as the sun rose and thought she felt herself dissolving into foam. Then she realised she was being drawn up into the air, surrounded by hundreds of transparent beautiful creatures. The little mermaid saw that her body had become just like theirs. 'Where am I?' she asked, and realised she had a voice; a voice that was like a song.

'You are with the daughters of the air,' the creatures answered. 'A mermaid can only gain an immortal soul if she wins the love of a human being. But a daughter of the air can gain one through her good deeds. After we have striven to do good for three hundred years, we gain an immortal soul. You, poor mermaid, have tried with your whole heart to do good. You have suffered and endured and so you have joined the daughters of the air.'

The little mermaid looked up to the sun and felt her eyes filling with tears of joy. She saw the people on the ship looking for her. Unseen, she kissed the foreheads of the bride and the prince and then rose into the sky with the daughters of the air.

Sleeping Beauty

Once upon a time in a faraway country there lived a king and queen. They lived in a beautiful castle and had many fine clothes, jewels and treasures. Although they had been married for many years, they were very sad, as they had no children.

One day, the queen was walking beside the river at the bottom of the garden. Suddenly, she saw a little fish that had thrown itself on the shore, gasping for air. Filled with pity, she picked it up and placed it back into the river. Before it swam away, the fish lifted its head out of the water and said, 'I know what you wish for and it shall come true. You will soon have a daughter.'

What the fish had foretold came to pass and the queen had a little girl. The king was overjoyed and announced a great feast to celebrate. He invited all his friends and kinsmen, as well as all the nobles and members of the court.

As was the tradition, the queen invited the fairies so that they might bestow gifts on the new princess. There were eight fairies in the kingdom but the king and queen only had seven gold dishes for the fairies to eat from, so they were forced to leave one out.

At the end of the feast, the fairies presented the princess with their gifts. The first fairy said the princess would be the most beautiful girl in the world. The second fairy gave her wit and intelligence and the third bestowed gracefulness on her. The fourth said she should dance perfectly, the fifth that she would sing beautifully and the sixth that she would play all kinds of music flawlessly.

Suddenly, in a flash of lightning, the eighth fairy appeared. She was very angry that she had not been invited to the feast. Determined to have her revenge, she cried out, 'Here is my gift! In her sixteenth year, the king's daughter shall prick her finger with a spindle and fall down dead!'

The king and queen were horrified, but the seventh fairy stepped forward. 'I have not yet given my gift,' she said. 'This evil wish must be fulfilled but I can soften it. The princess will not die when the spindle wounds her but she will fall asleep. After one hundred years, the son of a king shall wake her.'

The king, hoping to save his daughter, issued a decree that all spindles should be immediately destroyed and banned them from his entire kingdom. As the princess grew up, the gifts of the first six fairies all came true. The princess was beautiful, good and wise and everyone who knew her loved her.

One day, when the princess was in her sixteenth year, the king and queen went away on a royal visit, leaving the princess behind in the castle. She roved around the castle, exploring every room, tower and apartment. Finally, she came to a little room at the top of a tower, where she found a good old woman sitting at a spinning wheel with her spindle.

'Good mother, what are you doing there?' asked the princess.
She had never seen a spinning wheel before because they had all
been destroyed.

'I am spinning flax, my child,' said the old lady.

'How prettily the wheel spins around!' exclaimed the princess.
'May I have a try?'

But no sooner did the princess pick up the spindle than she pricked herself with it and fell down in a deep sleep. The old lady cried out for help and people came rushing from all quarters. They shook the princess, they threw cold water upon her face, they tried everything they could to wake her but still she slumbered.

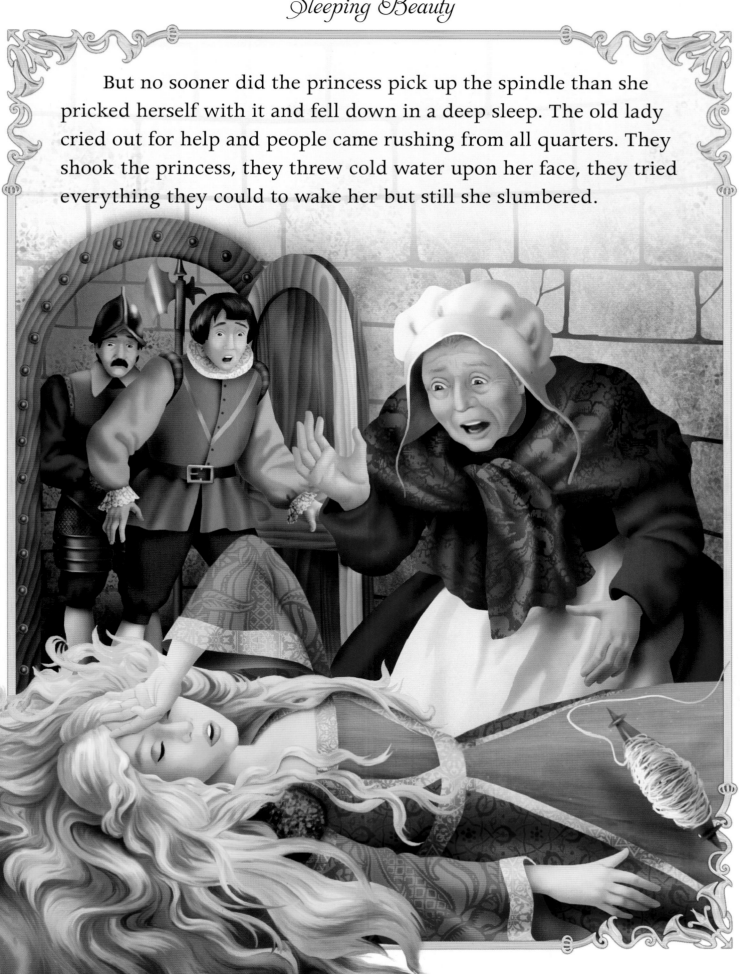

The king and queen rushed home to their daughter's side. Remembering the fairy's prediction, they ordered that the princess be laid out in the finest apartment in the palace on a bed embroidered with gold and silver thread. Despairing of ever seeing her awake again, the king sorrowfully commanded that all should leave the princess and let her sleep in peace.

Now the good fairy who had saved the princess's life was far away in another country, but when she heard the news, she set off at once to the palace in a chariot of fire drawn by dragons. The king met her and helped her down from the chariot. The fairy approved of all the arrangements but realised that if the poor princess slept for one hundred years, she would wake up orphaned and alone, surrounded by strangers.

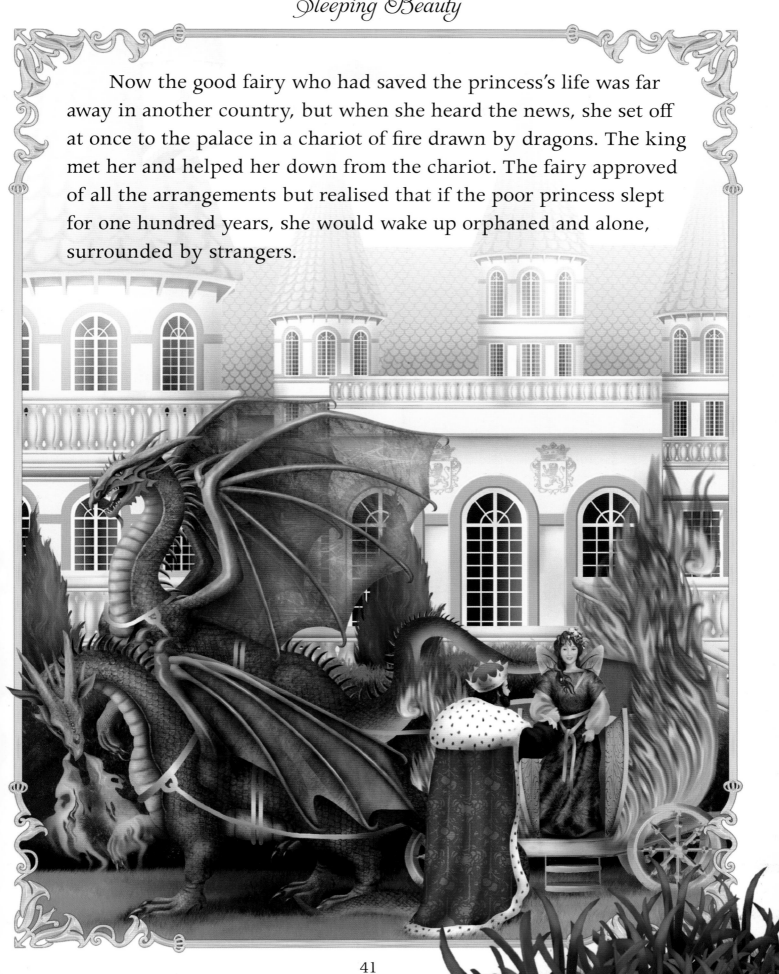

So the good fairy touched everything in the palace with her wand: the king and queen; the ministers of state; the members of the court; the maids of honour and the gentlemen in waiting; the bishops and the clergy; the governesses and the professors; the guards and the footmen; the pages and the heralds; the stewards and the cooks; and even the horses in the stables, the dogs in the yard and the princess's little pet puppy.

As soon as the fairy's wand touched them, everyone fell asleep, ready to wake with the princess. The spits in the kitchen stopped turning and the clocks stopped ticking and the whole castle slept. Then the fairy caused a great forest of thick trees, brambles and thorns to grow up around the castle so that only the very top of the towers could be seen and no one could come near. The castle lay quiet and undisturbed for years and years and eventually everyone forgot that it existed and who had lived there.

When a hundred years had passed, a prince was out hunting nearby. During the chase, he saw the thick wood and asked, 'What is this wood and what are those towers I can see appearing in the midst of it?'

No one could answer him. Some said that it was an old ruin, haunted by ghosts. Others said that a great ogre lived there and still others that it was the home of a band of evil witches.

Finally, an old woodcutter told the prince of a tale that he had heard from his grandfather. 'If it may please Your Highness,' said the old woodcutter, 'my grandfather used to say that in the forest is an enchanted castle. In this castle sleeps a beautiful princess, waiting for a prince to wake her.'

Hearing this, the prince was determined to explore the castle. He pushed his way through the trees and brambles of the thick forest. To his surprise, the bushes parted easily and the prince was able to make his way through, but when his men tried to follow, the trees closed in behind him, blocking their way.

Finally, the thick forest gave way and the prince found himself at the gates of a huge castle. He walked through the massive front gate and entered a wide open yard, where he was first struck with fear. Littered around the courtyard were the bodies of men and horses. However, looking closer, he saw that their faces were rosy and pink and their chests rose and fell as they slumbered.

Continuing on, the prince entered a court paved with marble, where he found rows of guards standing at attention, all asleep. He entered the throne room and saw the king and queen asleep on their thrones. The ministers of state were slumbering at their desks, pens in hand. All their clothes were as fresh as the day they had been washed and there was no dust or cobwebs to be seen.

As he wandered, the prince found rooms filled with lords and ladies, some standing, some sitting, but all asleep. Seamstresses were asleep over their sewing, cooks were sleeping over their pots and maids slumbered leaning on their brooms. He came to a grand staircase and made his way up, where he found apartments and rooms filled with sleeping people.

Finally, he came to the most grand apartment of all. Opening the door, he entered a room and found a bed beautifully embroidered with gold and silver thread. Lying on it was the most beautiful girl he'd ever seen. Her face was fresh and rosy, as though she had only just fallen asleep.

Trembling, the prince approached the bed and knelt beside her. He gazed at her lovely face a while, then lifted her white hand to his lips and gently kissed it.

At this, the long enchantment was broken. The princess opened her eyes and smiled at him. 'You have been a long while coming, my prince,' she said. The prince was charmed by these words and swore he loved her more than anything. The happy couple talked together for many hours, although the prince did not tell her that her dress was one hundred years out of fashion.

Meanwhile, the rest of the castle awakened. The prince and princess made their way down the great stairs, where the princess was happily reunited with her parents. A great feast was proclaimed, as everyone who had not just fallen in love was very hungry.

The great forest surrounding the castle disappeared as soon as the princess woke up. The whole country celebrated as the prince and princess were married in the castle. The good fairy blessed them and they lived happily ever after.

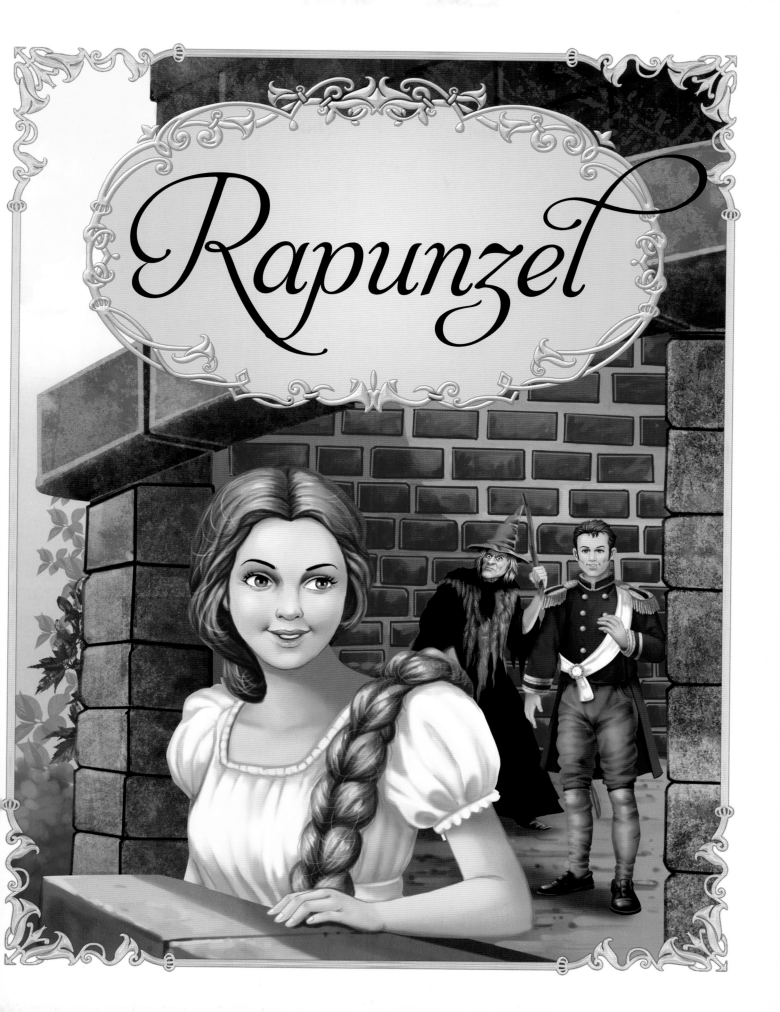

Rapunzel

Once upon a time there lived a couple who were going to have a child. They had a little window at the back of their house that looked out onto a lovely garden. The garden was surrounded by a high wall and no one dared enter it, for it belonged to a powerful Witch.

One day, the wife stood at the window and saw a garden bed full of the finest lettuce. When she realised she couldn't have any, she pined away and became pale and weak.

'Oh,' she moaned, 'if I can't have some lettuce to eat from the garden, I shall die.'

The man, who loved her dearly, thought, 'I should fetch her some lettuce, no matter what the cost.'

At sunset, the husband climbed over the wall into the Witch's garden. He quickly gathered a handful of lettuce leaves and returned with them to his wife. They tasted so good that her longing for the forbidden food grew stronger than ever. If she were to have any peace of mind, her husband would have to fetch her some more.

When the sun set, he climbed over the wall. Then he drew back in terror, for standing before him was the old Witch.

'How dare you steal my lettuce like a common thief?' she demanded. 'You shall suffer for your foolhardiness!'

'Please, spare me!' he implored. 'My wife saw your lettuce from her window. She had such a desire for it that she would certainly have died if she could not have a taste.'

Then the Witch grew a little less angry. She said, 'If that's so, you may take as much lettuce as you like, but on one condition: you will give me your child when it is born. I will look after it like a mother.' In his terror, the man agreed.

As soon as the child was born, it was taken away by the Witch. She named the girl Rapunzel, which is the name of the lettuce the child's mother so desired. Rapunzel was the most beautiful child under the sun. When she was twelve years old, the Witch shut her up in a tower in the middle of a great wood. The tower had no stairs or doors and only a small window at the very top. When the Witch wanted to get in, she stood under the window and called out:

'Rapunzel, Rapunzel, let down your hair.'

Rapunzel had beautiful, long hair as fine as spun gold. When she heard the Witch calling, she let her braid of hair fall down and the old Witch climbed up it to the top of the tower.

One day, a few years later, a Prince was riding through the wood. As he approached the tower, he heard someone singing so beautifully that he stopped and listened, entranced. It was Rapunzel, who, in her loneliness, passed the time by singing songs, her lovely voice ringing out into the forest.

The Prince longed to see who was singing, but there was no door in the tower. He was so captivated that he returned to the wood every day. One day, he was listening from behind a tree when he saw the old Witch. He heard her call out:

'Rapunzel, Rapunzel, let down your hair.'

Rapunzel let down her hair and the Witch climbed up. 'If that's the way into the tower, I'll try my luck,' thought the Prince.

The next day at sunset, the Prince went to the foot of the tower and cried out:

'Rapunzel, Rapunzel, let down your hair.'

As soon as Rapunzel let it down, the Prince climbed up.

At first Rapunzel was terribly frightened by this young man she had never met before. However, the Prince spoke to her kindly and gently. He told her that his heart had been so touched by her singing that he could not rest until he had met her. Very soon Rapunzel forgot her fear.

The Prince visited her often. When he asked her to marry him, she said, 'I will gladly marry you, only how am I to get out of the tower?' She thought for a moment and said, 'Every time you visit, bring a skein of silk. I will make a ladder. When it is finished, I will climb down and you can take me away on your horse.'

The Prince visited every evening because the Witch came during the day. The Witch knew nothing about this until one day Rapunzel, not thinking, asked the Witch, 'Why are you so much harder to pull up than the Prince? He is always with me in a moment.'

'Wicked child!' cried the Witch. 'I thought I had hidden you from the whole world, yet you have still managed to trick me!'

She grabbed Rapunzel's beautiful hair and picked up a pair of scissors. Snip! Snap! Off it came! The beautiful golden plait lay on the floor. The Witch was so cruel that she sent Rapunzel to a lonely desert to live in misery.

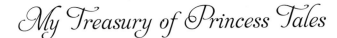

That evening, the Witch fastened the braid of hair to a hook in the window. The Prince came and called out:

'Rapunzel, Rapunzel, let down your hair!'

The Witch threw the plait down, and the Prince climbed up. Instead of his dear Rapunzel, he found the old Witch, laughing mockingly, 'Ha ha! You thought to find a pretty bird but she has flown away and won't sing any more! You will never see her again!'

The Prince was overcome with grief. In his despair, he jumped from the tower. He escaped with his life, but he fell in a thorn bush. The sharp thorns pierced his eyes and he could no longer see.

The Prince wandered, blind and miserable, through the forest. He ate nothing but roots and berries, and wept and mourned the loss of his beloved bride. He wandered like this from place to place for many years, as wretched and unhappy as it was possible to be.

At last, the poor blind Prince wandered to the desert where Rapunzel was living. He was roaming about in despair when he suddenly heard a familiar voice singing. The Prince eagerly followed the lovely sound, and when he was quite close, Rapunzel saw him and recognised him.

Rapunzel threw her arms around the Prince's neck and wept for joy at seeing him again and for sorrow at his poor sightless eyes. But then two of her tears fell into his eyes. Immediately, the Prince's eyes became clear and he could see as well as he had ever done.

The Prince led Rapunzel to his kingdom, where they were received and welcomed with great joy and relief. They were married and lived happily ever after.

Cinderella

Once upon a time there lived a gentleman with his young daughter. His wife had passed away, but their daughter had inherited her mother's rare goodness and sweetness of temper.

After several years had passed, the gentleman decided to marry again. Unhappily, his choice of bride was a poor one, for the lady he married was the proudest and most haughty woman imaginable. She had two daughters of her own, who were like her in every way.

The wedding was barely over when the woman's temper began to show. She could not bear the sweetness of the young girl, as it made her own daughters seem even worse. The stepmother gave her the dirtiest, hardest work in the house to do. Every day, she had to scour the dishes, clean the tables, polish the grates, scrub the floors and dust the bedrooms.

The poor girl was forced to sleep in the cold, bare attic on a pile of straw, while her two stepsisters slept in luxurious beds in fine bedrooms lined with mirrors so they could see their fine clothes. The young girl only had a plain shabby cotton dress to wear.

The girl bore all this patiently and did not even complain to her father, who was completely ruled by his wife, as she did not wish to add to his unhappiness. When her work was done, she would sit in the corner next to the chimney among the cinders. Her stepsisters mocked her and called her 'Cinderella'. However, despite her poor clothes and her daily toil, Cinderella was a hundred times more lovely than her stepsisters, despite their fine clothes.

It came to pass that the king's son came of age. A grand ball was announced in his honour and the most important and fashionable people in the town were invited. When their invitation arrived, the stepsisters immediately busied themselves with choosing their gowns, petticoats and jewellery for the occasion. Poor Cinderella spent her days lacing corsets, ironing dresses, picking up discarded clothes, sewing and shopping. The sisters instructed her to style their hair and paint their faces in different ways to see what looked best.

On the night of the ball, Cinderella busily dressed the stepsisters. They taunted her, saying, 'Cinderella, don't you wish that you were going to the ball?'

'Ah, you are laughing at me,' Cinderella sighed. 'It is not for such as I to think about going to balls.'

'You are right,' the stepsisters replied. 'How people would laugh to see a cinder wench dancing at a ball!'

With that, the two stepsisters climbed into their fine carriage and drove off to the ball. Cinderella watched until they were out of sight, and then sat in her corner next to the chimney and burst into tears.

Suddenly a kindly little old lady appeared out of nowhere in front of Cinderella, who was so startled that she stopped crying.

'Dear Cinderella, I am your godmother,' said the woman, who was a fairy. 'Why are you crying? Is it because you wish you could go to the ball?'

'Yes, indeed Godmother!' exclaimed Cinderella.

'Well, do what I say and I shall send you there,' said the fairy godmother. 'But first, I must get you ready. Run to the garden and fetch me a pumpkin.'

Cinderella ran out the kitchen door and soon came back with the largest pumpkin she could find. Her fairy godmother laid it on the ground and tapped it with her wand. The simple pumpkin turned into a beautiful coach made of the finest gold.

Next, the fairy godmother looked in the mousetrap in the pantry and saw that six mice were caught there, poking their noses through the bars. As she freed each mouse, the fairy tapped it with her wand. Each mouse turned into a handsome coach horse, with an elegant long neck, a sweeping tail and a lovely mouse-grey coat.

Then the fairy directed Cinderella to the garden, where she found six lizards. They were soon transformed into six footmen, all wearing shining green and silver coats.

Finally, Cinderella was sent to look in the rat trap. She returned with a great rat with a long beard. One wave of the fairy godmother's wand and the rat turned into a jolly coachman with the finest whiskers imaginable.

'Well my dear, is this equipage fit for the ball?' asked the fairy godmother.

'Why yes!' exclaimed Cinderella. Then she paused and looked down at her shabby, dirty dress. 'But must I go as I am, wearing these rags?'

The fairy godmother touched Cinderella with her wand. Cinderella's shabby dress changed into a beautiful ball gown of gold and silver that sparkled with diamonds. On her feet she wore dainty slippers made of perfect glass.

'Now, my dear, you can go to the ball,' said the fairy godmother. 'Just remember one thing. You must leave before the clock strikes midnight, otherwise your dress will become rags again, your carriage a pumpkin, your horses mice, your footmen lizards and your coachman a rat.'

Cinderella promised she would leave before midnight and then climbed into her coach and drove away, her heart full of joy.

When she arrived at the ball, the whole palace was struck with how beautiful she was. As soon as he saw her, the prince was in love. He came forward and lead her into the ballroom and begged her to dance with him the whole evening. Everyone marvelled at her elegance and grace as she danced and all the ladies admired Cinderella's fine gown and imagined how they could have a dress made just like it.

When supper was served, the prince waited on her himself and was so enamoured that he could not eat. Cinderella saw her stepsisters looking at her in admiration, but when she spoke to them, they did not recognise her. Time passed quickly and soon Cinderella heard the clock chiming eleven and three quarters. She quickly made her exit and returned home.

Cinderella told her fairy godmother about her lovely evening and how the prince had begged her to return for the second night of the ball. As she was talking, she heard her stepsisters return home and ran to meet them, rubbing her eyes as though she had been sleeping.

'If you had been there, you would have seen such a sight!' exclaimed one sister. 'A beautiful princess attended. No one knows who she is but the prince is smitten and would give the world to know her name. How honoured we were when she spoke to us!'

'Oh I would so like to see her,' said Cinderella. 'Could you not lend me a dress so I could attend the ball, just to catch a glimpse?'

'Don't be ridiculous!' snapped the other sister. 'I would not be so silly as to lend my clothes to a cinder maid!' Cinderella was glad, as she had asked in jest and knew that she would be refused.

The next night, the two stepsisters attended the ball and so did Cinderella, dressed even more magnificently. The prince was constantly by her side and Cinderella so enjoyed his company that she did not notice how the time flew by.

Suddenly, Cinderella heard the clock start to strike twelve. She ran from the ballroom as fast as she could. The prince followed but he could not overtake her. As she ran, she left behind one of her glass slippers on the palace stairs. When Cinderella got home, her clothes had returned to rags but she was clutching the other glass slipper.

The stepsisters returned soon after and Cinderella asked them how they had enjoyed the ball and if the mysterious princess had attended. They replied that she had, but when the clock struck twelve, the princess had run from the ballroom in such haste that she had left behind one of her glass slippers. The prince had picked it up and spent the rest of the ball gazing at it, so in love was he.

A few days later, it was proclaimed that the prince would marry whoever could perfectly fit the glass slipper. All the ladies of the court and palace tried on the slipper, but none could fit into it. It was laid upon a silk cushion and taken to all the ladies of the town for them to try, but to no avail.

When it came to the house of the stepsisters, they tried all they could to fit their feet into the slipper. They pushed and shoved and curled their toes, but the slipper was too small and dainty for them.

'Let me try,' said Cinderella.

The two sisters laughed at her and began to tease her, but the courtier who had been sent with the slipper said that he had orders that every woman must try it on. He slipped the slipper on her foot and found that it fitted as perfectly as if it had been made for her.

As the astonished stepsisters looked on, the fairy godmother appeared and waved her wand and they saw before them the beautiful lady from the ball. They threw themselves before Cinderella and begged her to forgive them. Cinderella was so good that she bade them rise and embraced them.

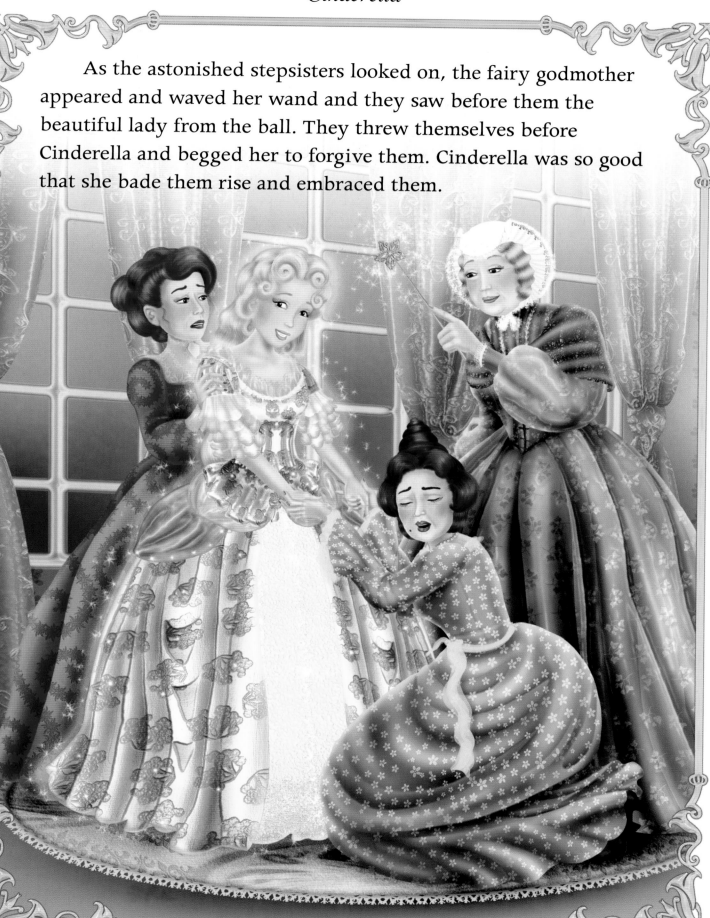

Cinderella was taken to the prince. When he saw her, the prince thought Cinderella was more beautiful than ever and he fell to his knees and asked her to marry him. A few days later they were married and they lived happily ever after.

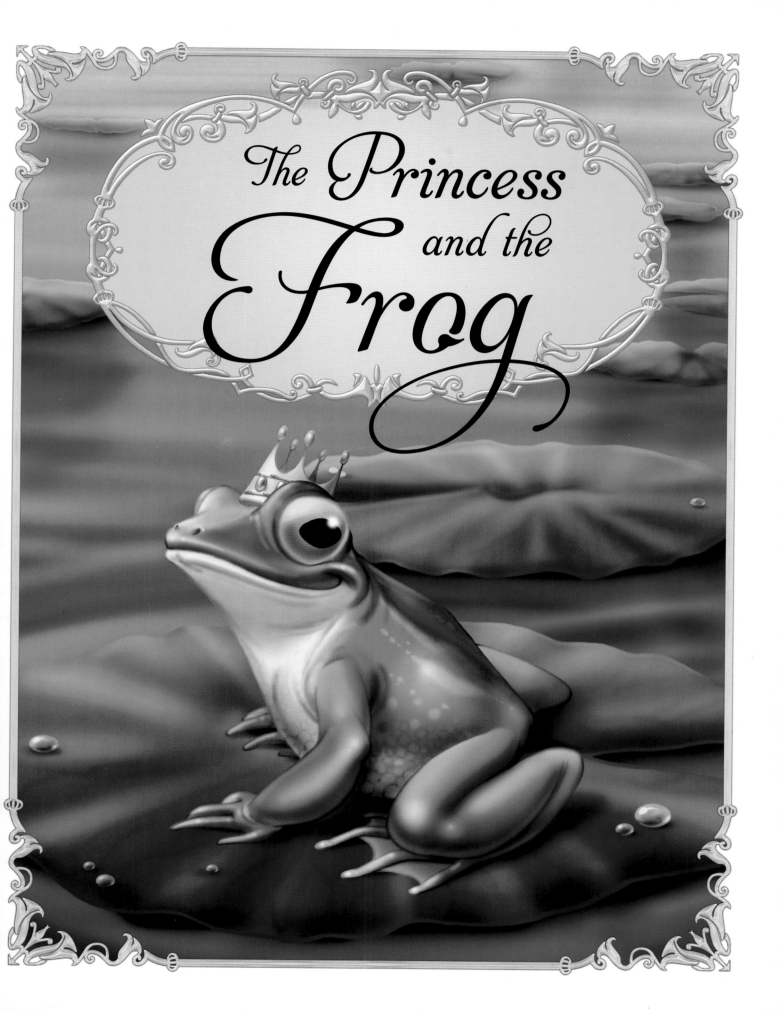

The Princess and the Frog

Once upon a time, there lived a king. His daughters were all beautiful, but the youngest was the most beautiful of all. A great forest lay next to the king's castle and in that forest was a deep well. On hot days, the youngest daughter would go to the forest and sit under a tree next to the well to play in the cool shade. The young princess's favourite plaything was a lovely golden ball, and there she would sit, tossing her ball in the air and catching it.

Alas, one day as she was sitting by the well, the princess threw her golden ball so high that instead of falling into her outstretched hand, it bounced away and rolled across the grass into the depths of the well. The princess ran to the side of the well, but she looked for her ball in vain, as the well was so deep that no one could see the bottom. The young princess began to weep at the loss of her favourite toy and could find no comfort.

As she sat crying, the young princess heard someone call out to her. 'Why do you weep so, princess?' said the voice. 'You cry so hard that you would even break the heart of a stone.'

The princess looked up to see where the voice was coming from and saw that a frog had lifted his ugly head out of the well and was talking to her.

'Alas, nasty frog,' she replied, 'I am weeping for my lovely golden ball. It has fallen into the well and is lost. Oh, what I would give to get it back!'

'Do not cry princess,' replied the slimy frog. 'I can help you, but what would you give me if I bring your ball back to you?'

'Whatever you ask for, dear frog,' said the princess. 'I would give all my fine clothes, my jewels, my pearls and even the precious golden crown on my head if I could get my ball back!'

'I care not for fine clothes, jewels, pearls or golden crowns,' answered the frog. 'But if you will love me and let me be your friend and playmate, and sit by you at your little table, and eat off your golden plate and drink out of your golden cup, and sleep on your pillow in your bed – if you will promise me this – then I will bring you back your golden ball from the depths of the well.'

'Oh yes!' cried the princess. 'If you will bring me my ball back, I promise I will do all you ask!'

But the princess was really thinking, 'How silly this frog is! All he can do is sit in the well with the other frogs and croak all day long. He's not fit to be anybody's playmate!'

So the frog dived down deep into the well. After a while, he swam back up to the surface again, holding the princess's golden ball in his mouth. He threw the ball over the edge of the well on to the grass and the princess ran and joyfully picked it up.

The princess was so happy to have her ball back that she ran away merrily, giving no thought to the frog and her promise.

'Wait princess! Don't forget your promise!' cried the frog. 'Take me with you! I cannot run as fast as you!'

But the princess did not hear the cries of the frog as she ran home to the castle. The poor frog was left to dive sadly back into the well.

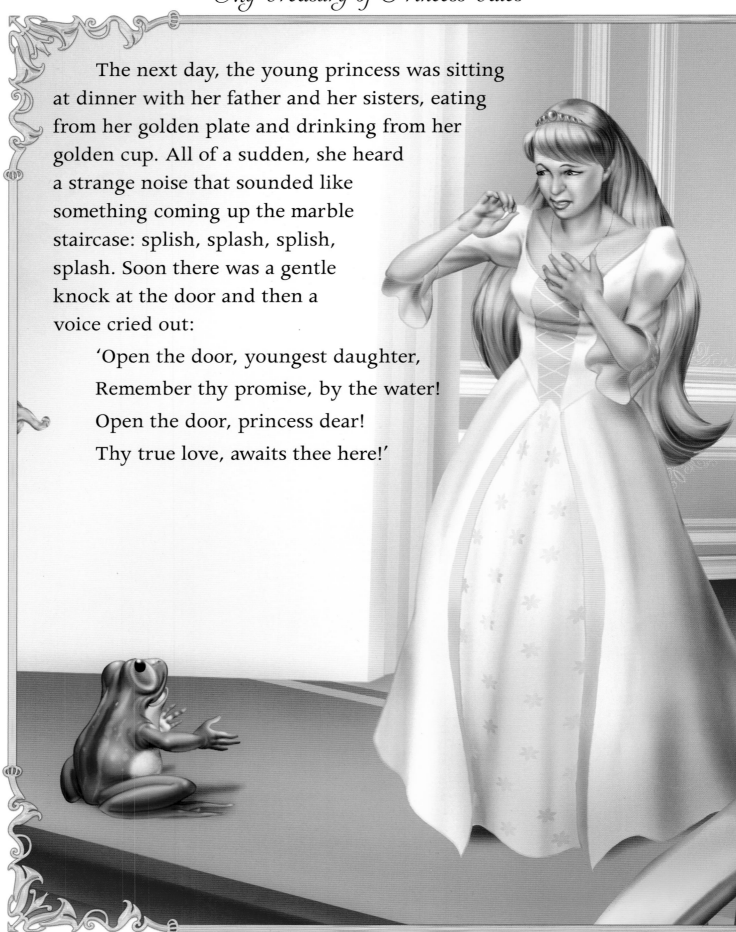

The next day, the young princess was sitting at dinner with her father and her sisters, eating from her golden plate and drinking from her golden cup. All of a sudden, she heard a strange noise that sounded like something coming up the marble staircase: splish, splash, splish, splash. Soon there was a gentle knock at the door and then a voice cried out:

'Open the door, youngest daughter,
Remember thy promise, by the water!
Open the door, princess dear!
Thy true love, awaits thee here!'

The princess ran to the door to see who was there, but when she opened it, she saw the frog from the well sitting there. She slammed the door in fright and ran back to the table.

However, her father saw that something had frightened her and so he asked her, 'What ails you my daughter? Has some beast come to carry you away?'

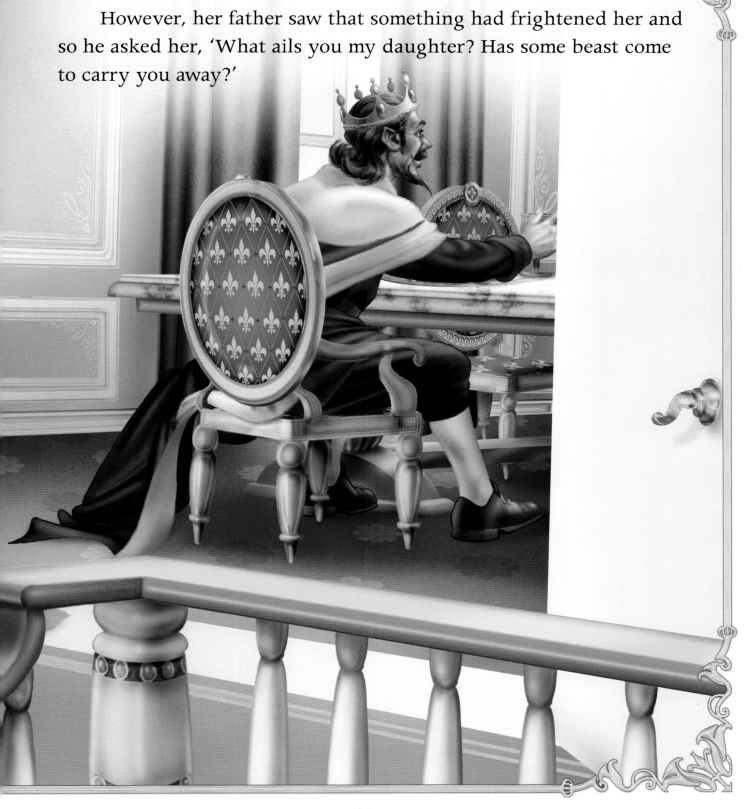

'It is no beast, father,' the young princess explained. 'It is nothing but an ugly frog.'

'A frog?' asked the surprised king. 'What does a frog want with you?'

'Yesterday I was playing with my golden ball near the well,' the princess replied. 'It fell in the water and I couldn't get it out because the well is so deep. However, this frog fetched it for me after I promised that he could be my companion. I never thought he would leave the well, but here he is at the door, knocking to come in.'

Again there was a knock at the door, and again the frog cried out:

'Open the door, youngest daughter,

Remember thy promise, by the water!

Open the door, princess dear!

Thy true love, awaits thee here!'

The king turned to his daughter and said, 'As you have given your promise, you must keep your word. Do not refuse to help someone who has helped you. Go and let the frog in.'

So the princess opened the door and let the frog in. He hopped along behind her, following her back to her place at the table.

'Lift me up so I may eat off your golden plate and drink out of your golden cup!' the frog cried.

The princess tried to resist, but her father commanded her to keep her promise. 'You must keep your promise, daughter,' said the king.

So the princess lifted the frog up on to the table, where he ate from her golden plate and sipped from her golden cup. The frog ate well, but the princess hardly touched a morsel, so disgusted and upset was she.

Then the frog said, 'Now princess, I am tired. Carry me upstairs to your room and let me sleep next to you in your bed.'

The princess began to cry, as she hated the thought of the nasty frog asleep in her pretty silk sheets, but her father looked at her angrily and again said, 'As you have given your promise, you must keep your word. Do not forget your pledge. Remember, he helped you when you were in trouble.'

So the young princess carried the frog upstairs to her bedroom and laid him on her pillow, where he slept all night. As soon as the sun rose, the frog hopped downstairs and went back to the well.

'At last he is gone,' thought the relieved princess, 'and I shall hear from him no more.'

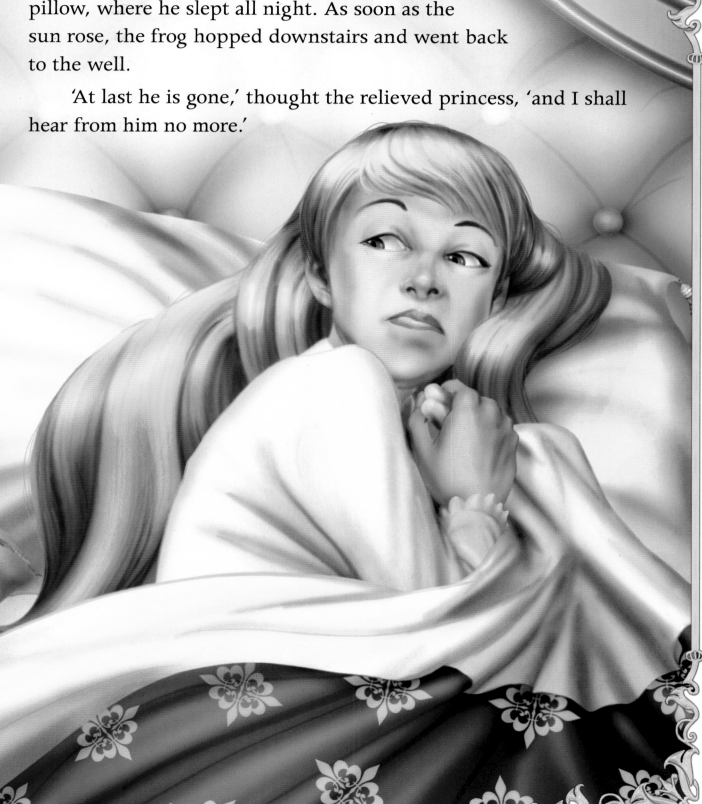

But the next evening as she was sitting down to dinner, the young princess again heard a gentle knock at the door and a voice crying out:

'Open the door, youngest daughter,

Remember thy promise, by the water!

Open the door, princess dear!

Thy true love, awaits thee here!'

Reluctantly, the princess let the frog dine with her and let him sleep on her pillow.

But she was becoming used to him now, and didn't find him quite so disgusting. After all, he was a polite frog, with good manners and lovely kind eyes. Again at sunrise, the frog hopped downstairs back to the well, and the princess found she actually missed his company.

The princess was not surprised to hear another knock at the door on the third night and a voice crying out:

'Open the door, youngest daughter,

Remember thy promise, by the water!

Open the door, princess dear!

Thy true love, awaits thee here!'

Again she dined with the frog, this time quite happily. She cheerfully chatted with him as they ate and carried him up to her room where again he slept on her pillow.

Imagine her surprise the next morning as the sun was rising when she woke. The princess was astonished to see, instead of a frog, a handsome prince standing next to her bed looking down on her with kind and beautiful eyes.

The handsome prince told her that he had been cursed by an evil witch, who had changed him into a frog. He was destined to stay a frog forever, unless a beautiful princess would let him eat from her plate and sleep on her pillow for three nights in a row.

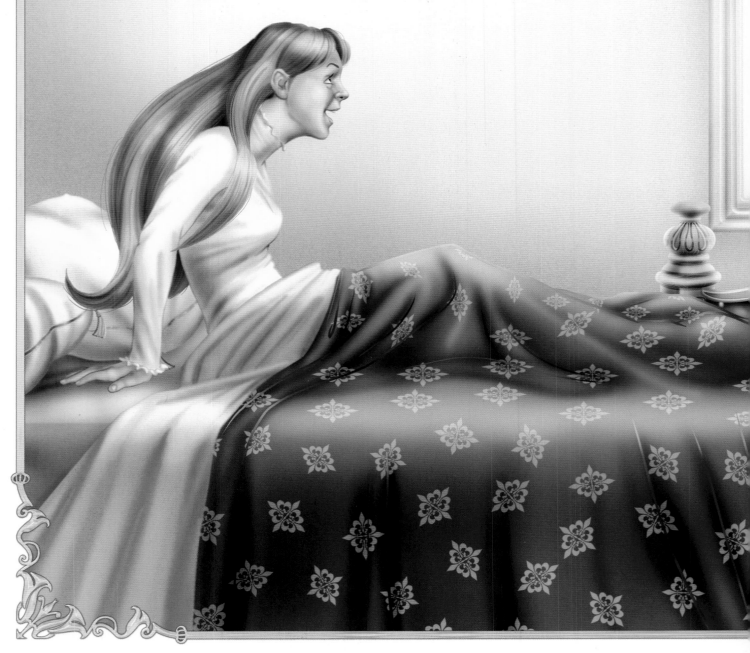

'You have broken the evil spell,' the handsome prince said. 'Come with me to my father's kingdom and marry me and I will love you as long as you live.'

The young princess was overjoyed and accepted his hand in marriage.

As they spoke together, a golden carriage drove up outside, pulled by eight powerful horses decked with feathers and a golden harness. Behind the coach was the prince's servant Faithful Henry, who had been so unhappy when his dear master had been turned into a frog by the witch that his heart had nearly broken.

Faithful Henry helped the prince and princess into the carriage and drove them to the prince's kingdom.

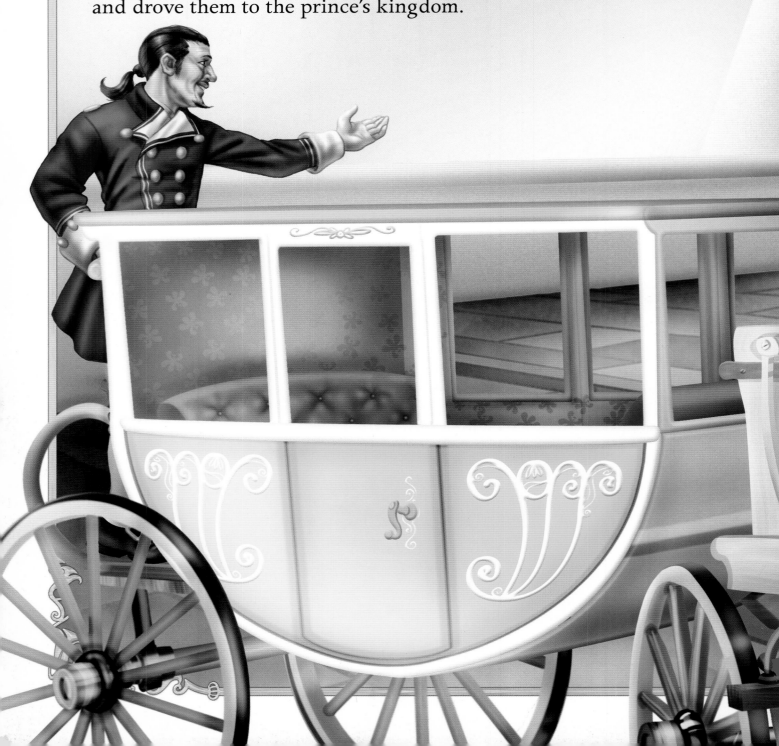

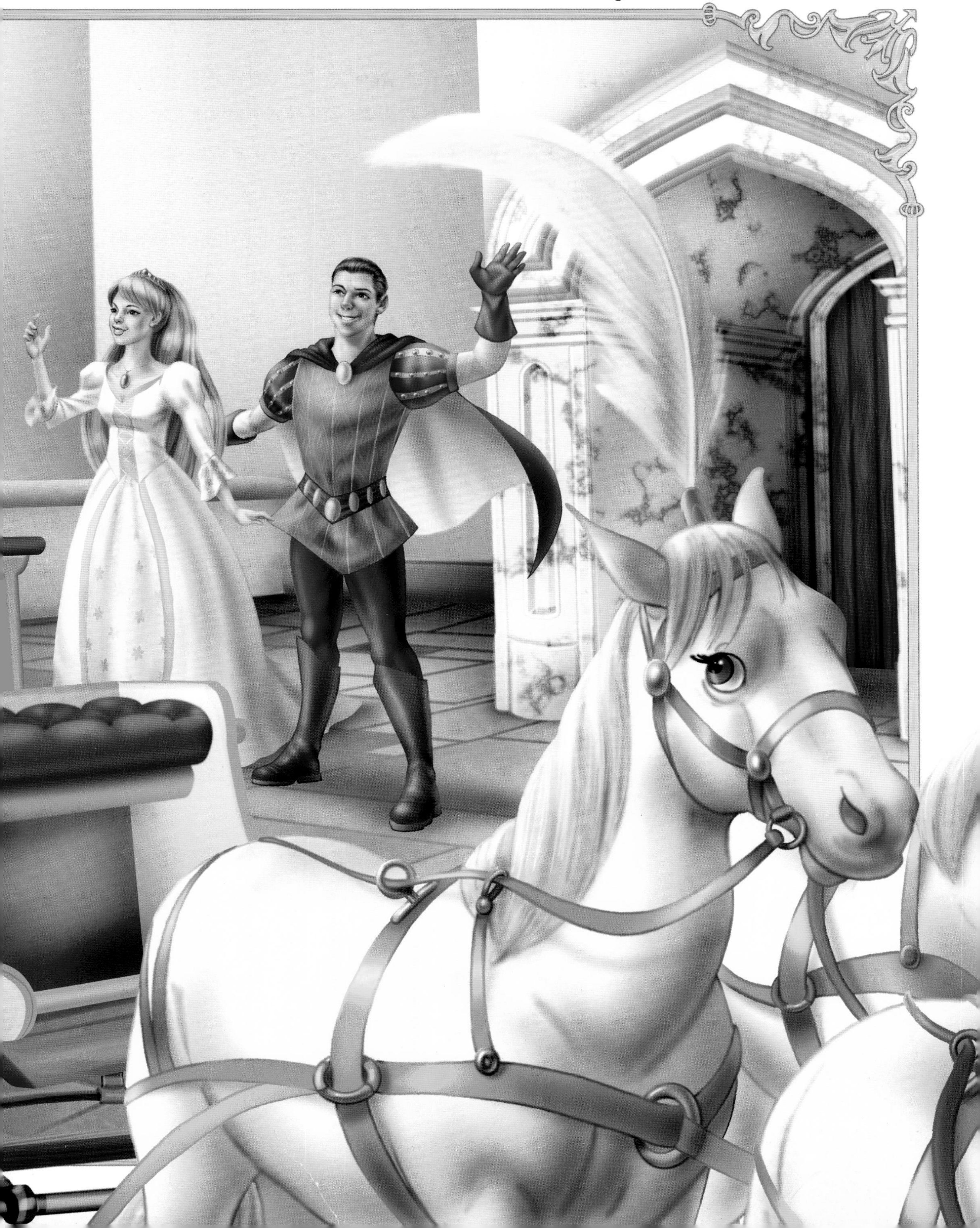

As they drove away, they heard the sound of Faithful Henry singing at the top of his voice, so overjoyed was he that his master was free and happy. When they reached the kingdom, the prince and the princess were married and lived happily ever after.

Thumbelina

There was once a woman who wished to have a child. She went to a fairy, and said, 'I would like to have a child so much. Can you help me?'

'Oh, that is easy,' said the fairy. 'Here is some special barley. Put it into a flower-pot and see what happens.'

The woman went home and planted the barley. Immediately a handsome flower grew, its petals tightly closed like a bud. As the woman watched in astonishment, the flower opened to reveal a graceful little maiden. She was barely half as long as a thumb, so the woman named her Thumbelina. Her bed was a walnut shell with a violet-petal mattress and a rose-petal quilt.

One night, a large, ugly toad crept through the window and saw Thumbelina sleeping in her walnut shell. 'What a pretty little wife for my son,' said the toad, and she took the shell to the stream where she lived with her son.

'We will put her on a water-lily leaf in the middle of the stream so she won't escape,' said the toad to her son. When Thumbelina woke the next morning she began to cry, for she did not know where she was or how to get home.

The old toad swam out to the leaf with her ugly son and said, 'Here is my son. He will be your husband.'

Then they left Thumbelina alone on the water-lily leaf, where she sat and wept. She could not bear to think of life with the ugly toad.

The fish in the stream felt sorry that Thumbelina should have to live with the ugly toads so they surrounded the stalk of the leaf and gnawed it through. The water-lily leaf floated down the stream carrying Thumbelina to faraway lands. Thumbelina was glad, for the toad could not reach her now. She lived by the river and the birds sweetly sang to her.

Summer and autumn passed and then came the long, cold winter. The birds who had sung to her flew away, and the trees and flowers withered. She was dreadfully cold, for her clothes were torn. It began to snow and she shivered with cold and hunger.

One day, while searching for food, Thumbelina came to the cottage of a field-mouse. She knocked on the door.

'You poor little creature,' said the field-mouse when she saw the starving girl. 'Come in and share my dinner.' She quickly came to like Thumbelina and said, 'You can stay with me all winter if you keep my rooms clean.' Thumbelina agreed and was very happy.

'My neighbour is a very rich mole,' said the field-mouse. 'If you had him for a husband you would be well provided for.'

The mole was indeed rich, but he was also quite disagreeable and did not like the sun. The field-mouse insisted Thumbelina sing to him, and the mole fell in love with her sweet voice. He dug a passage from the field-mouse's house to his burrow and encouraged them to visit whenever they liked.

One evening, the mole and Thumbelina were walking together when they came upon a swallow that had died of cold. The mole said, 'How miserable it must be to be a bird! They do nothing but sing in the summer and die of hunger in the winter.'

Thumbelina said nothing. 'Perhaps this bird sang to me sweetly in the summer,' she thought.

That night Thumbelina could not sleep, so she got out of bed and wove a carpet of hay. She carried it to the bird and spread it over him so that he might lie warmly in the cold earth. 'Farewell, pretty bird,' she said.

Thumbelina laid her head on the bird's breast and was surprised when his heart went 'thump, thump'. He was not dead, only numb from the cold and the warm carpet had restored him to life.

The next morning Thumbelina stole out to see him. He was very weak and could barely open an eye to look at her.

'Stay in your warm bed and I will take care of you,' she said. With much care and love Thumbelina nursed him in secret for the whole winter.

When spring came, the swallow bade farewell to Thumbelina. He asked if she would go with him but Thumbelina knew it would make the field-mouse very sad if she left her and said, 'No, I cannot.'

'Farewell then, little maiden,' said the swallow and he flew out into the sunshine.

Soon afterwards, the field-mouse took Thumbelina aside and said, 'You are going to be married to the mole as soon as summer is over.' Thumbelina wept at the thought. Every morning and evening she crept out to see the blue sky. She wished to see her dear swallow again but he had flown far away.

The day approached when the mole was to take Thumbelina away to live with him. She went to say goodbye to the sun. 'Farewell bright sun,' she cried, curling her arm around a red flower. 'Greet the swallow for me, if you should see him again.'

Suddenly she heard a loud 'tweet, tweet!' from above. She looked up and saw the swallow. 'Winter is coming,' he said. 'Now will you fly with me to warmer lands?'

'I will,' said Thumbelina, and she climbed on to the bird's back. The swallow flew over forests and high above mountains, leaving the mole and the field-mouse far behind.

At last they came to a blue lake. Beside it, surrounded by flowers, stood a palace of white marble. The swallow laid Thumbelina gently in a beautiful blossom.

'I live in a nest beneath this castle's tallest turret but you shall live here,' said the swallow with a knowing smile.

On the flower stood a man, as tiny as Thumbelina, wearing a gold crown and delicate wings. A tiny man or woman lived in every flower and he was the King of them all. The little King thought her the prettiest maiden he had ever seen. He asked her to marry him and to be Queen of all the flowers.

Thumbelina happily agreed. For the wedding she was given a lovely pair of wings, which were fastened to her shoulders so she could fly from flower to flower as the little swallow sang a wedding song.

'Farewell, farewell,' said the swallow when it was time to return to the forest for summer.

There he had a nest over the window of a house where a writer of fairytales lived. The swallow sang, 'Tweet, tweet,' and from his song came this story.

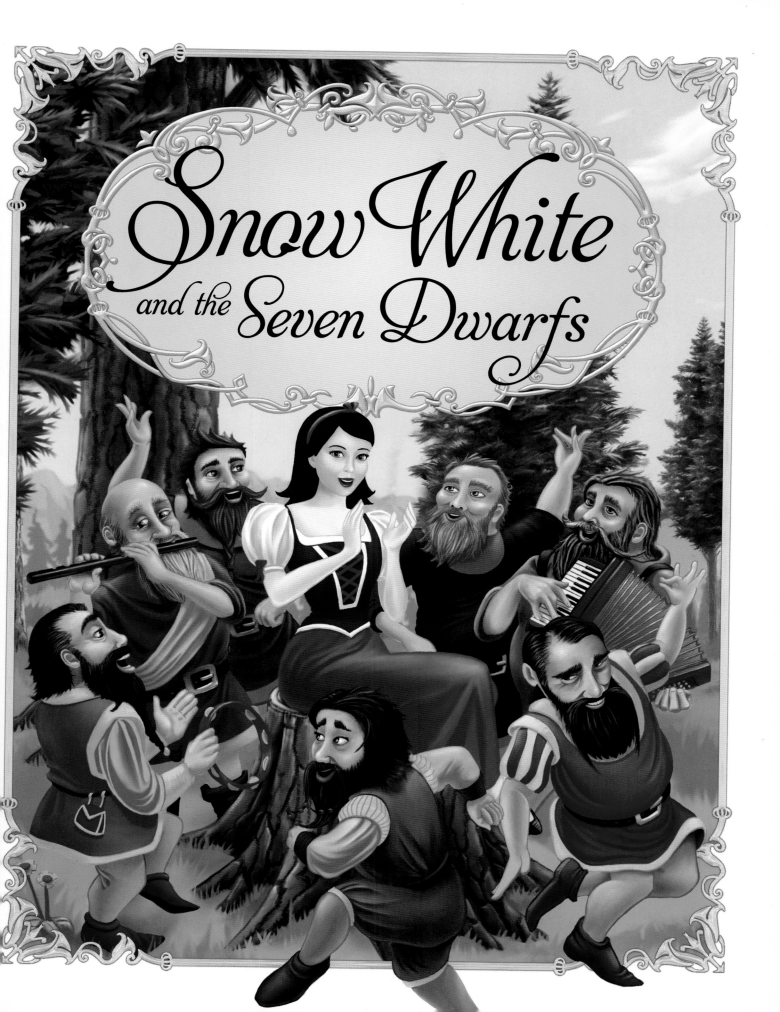

Snow White
and the Seven Dwarfs

Once upon a time, in the middle of winter when the snowflakes were falling from the sky, a queen sat sewing at her window, which had a frame of black ebony wood. As she sewed, she looked out at the snow and accidentally pricked her finger with the needle. Three drops of blood fell from the open window into the snow.

As she looked at the brilliant red on the white snow, the queen thought to herself, 'If only I had a child with skin as white as snow, with lips as red as blood and hair as black as ebony.'

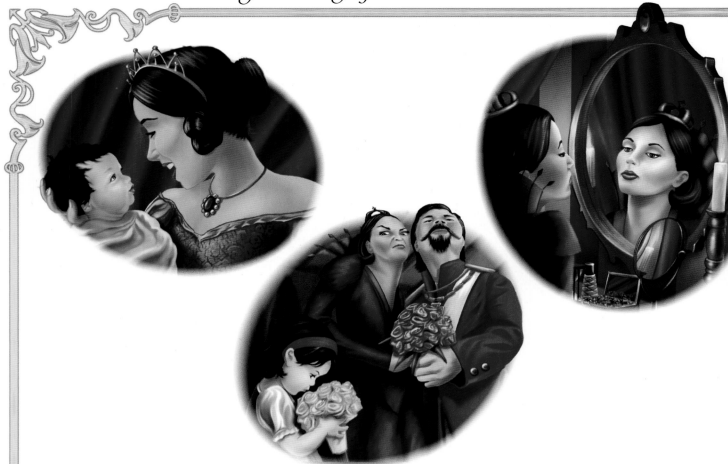

Soon after that, the queen had a little daughter. She was named Snow White, because her skin was as white as snow, her lips as red as blood and her hair as black as ebony. Alas, soon after the child was born, the queen died.

A year later, the king remarried. His new wife was a beautiful woman, but she was also proud and vain. She could not bear the thought that someone else might be more beautiful than her. She had a magic mirror which she looked into every morning, and asked:

'Mirror, mirror, on the wall,

Who in this land is the fairest of all?'

The mirror would always reply:

'You, Queen, are the fairest of all.'

The queen was always satisfied, because she knew that the mirror had to tell the truth.

As the years passed and Snow White grew up, she became more and more beautiful. Eventually, she was even more beautiful than the queen herself. One day, the queen asked her mirror:

'Mirror, mirror, on the wall,

Who in this land is the fairest of all?'

The mirror answered:

'You, my queen are fair, it's true,

But Snow White is a thousand times fairer than you.'

When the queen heard this, she turned white with fury and jealousy. From that time on, whenever the queen looked at Snow White, her heart heaved in her breast. So great was her hatred that she had no peace, day or night, and her envy and pride grew like a weed.

Finally, she summoned a huntsman and ordered, 'Take Snow White out into the woods. I never want to see her again. Kill her, and bring me her heart as proof she is dead!'

The huntsman took Snow White out into the woods. But when he drew his knife, Snow White begged him to spare her life. The huntsman took pity on her and could not bear to harm her. 'Run away, poor child,' he said to her.

'The wild animals will soon devour her,' the huntsman thought sadly, but he was relieved that he did not have to kill her. He spied a young boar in the forest and killed it, cut out its heart and took it back to the queen as proof of Snow White's death. The queen was very pleased.

Poor Snow White was all alone in the great forest. She looked around, and then she began to run. She ran over sharp stones and through thorn bushes and she saw wild animals, but she came to no harm.

Snow White ran for as long as she could, until it was almost evening. Then she saw a little cottage in the forest, so she went inside to rest. Everything in the cottage was very small but it was very neat and clean. There was a table set with seven places, all with little plates, mugs, spoons, knives and forks. A little loaf of bread sat on every plate and each little mug had some wine in it. Against the wall were seven little beds.

Snow White was so hungry and thirsty that she ate a piece of each loaf and drank some wine from each mug. After that, she tried all the beds, but some were too short and some were too hard, until she tried the seventh bed, which suited her very well. She lay down and fell asleep.

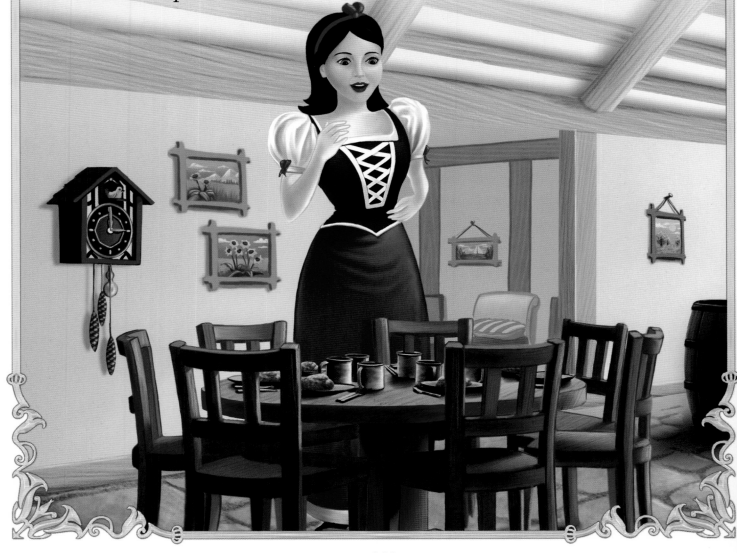

When it was dark outside, the owners of the cottage came home. They were seven dwarfs who dug and mined in the mountains for gold and silver. The dwarfs lit their seven candles and saw that someone had been in their house, for things had moved from where they left them.

The first cried, 'Who has been eating from my plate?'
The second cried, 'Who has been eating my bread?'
The third cried, 'Who has been sitting on my chair?'
The fourth cried, 'Who has been using my fork?'
The fifth cried, 'Who has been cutting with my knife?'
The sixth cried, 'Who has been meddling with my spoon?'
The seventh cried, 'Who has been drinking from my mug?'

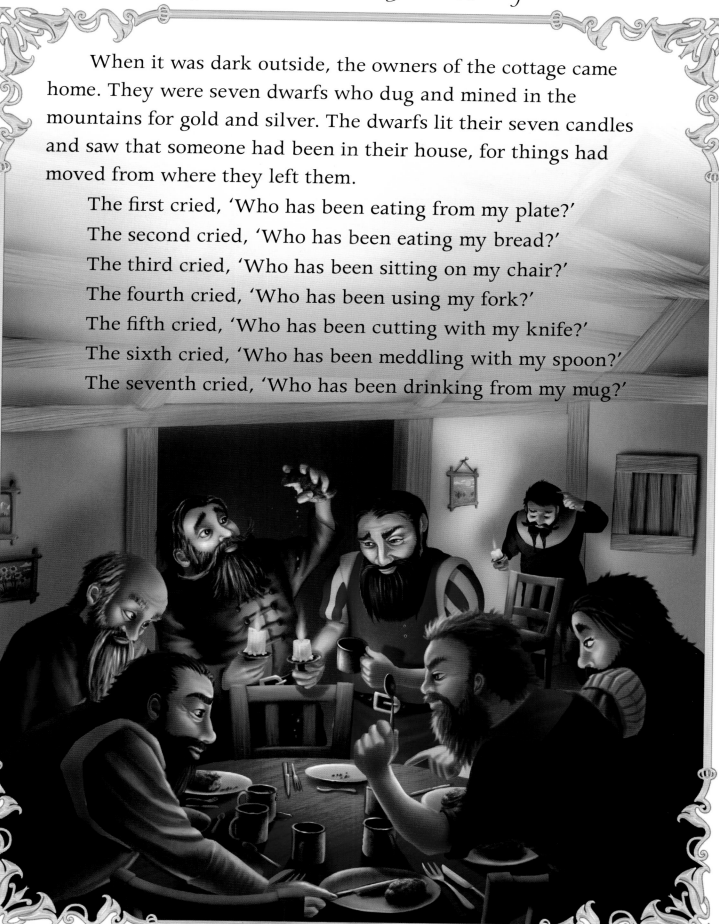

Then the first dwarf looked around and exclaimed, 'Who has been lying on my bed?'

The other dwarfs all cried out that someone had been lying on their beds too. But the seventh dwarf saw Snow White asleep on his bed and called the others to come and see her. They looked at her by the light of their seven candles and exclaimed, 'Good heavens! What a lovely girl she is!' They didn't wake her up but let her sleep through the night.

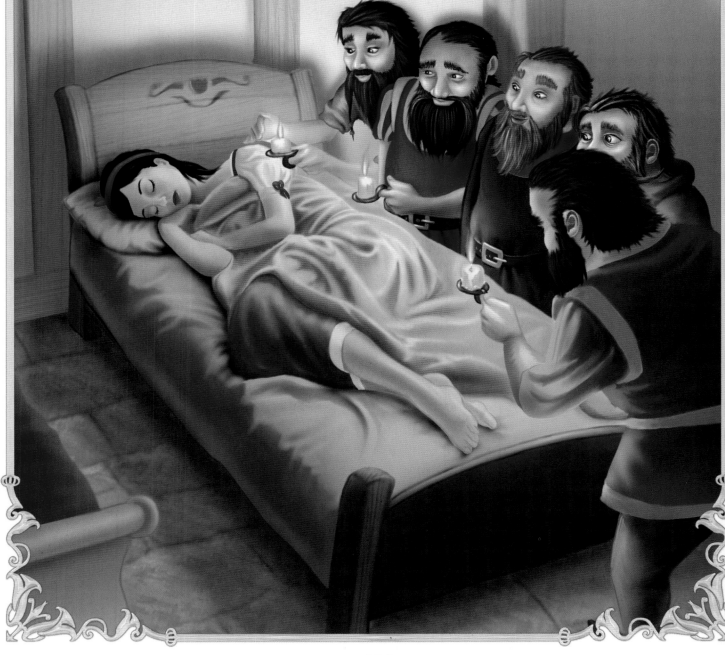

The next morning, Snow White woke up and saw the seven dwarfs. She was frightened, but soon realised they were friendly and introduced herself. She told them how her stepmother tried to kill her but the huntsman had spared her life and she had run until she found their cottage.

The dwarfs said, 'If you will keep house for us, you can live here and we will take care of you.' Snow White agreed with all her heart.

Each day, the dwarfs went to work in the mountains, digging for gold and silver, while Snow White stayed home alone. The dwarfs warned her, 'The queen will soon discover where you are. Make sure you don't let anyone in.'

The queen believed Snow White was dead and that she was the most beautiful again. She went to her magic mirror and asked:

'Mirror, mirror, on the wall,

Who in this land is the fairest of all?'

The mirror answered:

'You, my queen are fair, it's true,

But Snow White, beyond the mountains, with the seven dwarfs,

Is still a thousand times fairer than you.'

This upset the queen, as she realised that Snow White was still alive. She couldn't bear the thought that someone was more beautiful than her, so she dressed herself up as an old peddler woman. In this disguise, she went to the house of the seven dwarfs and knocked at the door. She called out, 'Beautiful wares for sale!'

Snow White looked out the window and asked what was for sale. 'Fine laces in all colours!' replied the old peddler.

'She looks like an honest woman,' thought Snow White, and she opened the door. She bought a pretty bodice lace.

'Let me lace you up,' said the disguised queen, but she pulled so hard that Snow White could not breathe and she fell down as though she were dead.

'You used to be more beautiful,' laughed the queen, and went on her way.

Soon after, the seven dwarfs came home. When they saw poor Snow White lying there, they lifted her up and saw the tight lace. They quickly cut it and Snow White began to breathe again. When the dwarfs heard what happened, they said to Snow White, 'That old peddler woman was no other than the queen! Make sure you let no one in when you are alone.'

When she got home, the queen went to her magic mirror and asked:

'Mirror, mirror, on the wall,

Who in this land is the fairest of all?'

The mirror answered:

'You, my queen are fair, it's true,

But Snow White, beyond the mountains, with the seven dwarfs,

Is still a thousand times fairer than you.'

The queen was furious that Snow White was still alive. Using her witchcraft, she made a poisoned comb. She disguised herself as another old woman and went to the dwarfs' house. She knocked at the door and called out, 'Fine wares for sale!'

Snow White looked out the window and said, 'I am not to let anyone in.'

'Surely you can take a look,' replied the old woman, pulling out the poisoned comb. Snow White liked it so much that she agreed and opened the door. The old woman offered to comb her hair, but as soon as the comb touched her, Snow White fell down unconscious.

'Now you are finished!' cried the queen, and went on her way.

Soon the seven dwarfs came home and saw Snow White lying on the ground as though dead. They pulled the poison comb out of her hair and Snow White awoke and told them what happened. Again, they warned her not to open the door to anyone.

The queen went home and again asked her magic mirror:

'Mirror, mirror, on the wall,

Who in this land is the fairest of all?'

The mirror answered:

'You, my queen are fair, it's true,

But Snow White, beyond the mountains, with the seven dwarfs,

Is still a thousand times fairer than you.'

The queen flew into a rage. 'Snow White shall die!' she shouted.

She went to her secret room and made a poisoned apple. It had beautiful red cheeks and an alluring smell. Anyone would be tempted to eat it. Disguising herself as a peasant woman, the queen went to the house of the seven dwarfs and knocked at the door.

Snow White looked out the window. When she saw the peasant woman, she said, 'I am not to let anyone in.'

'I don't mind,' said the peasant woman. 'Don't worry, I will easily be able to sell my apples in time. In fact, let me give you this pretty one as a gift.'

'I cannot accept anything,' replied Snow White.

'What are you afraid of?' asked the peasant woman. 'Here, I'll cut it in two. You can eat one half and I shall have the other.'

The queen had cleverly made the apple so that only half was poisoned. She cut it in two and ate some of the unpoisoned half.

Snow White longed for the apple, and when she saw the peasant woman eating it, she could no longer resist. She took the apple and bit into it, but she barely had it in her mouth before she fell down dead.

'This time the dwarfs can't wake you!' the queen laughed.

The queen went home and asked the magic mirror:

'Mirror, mirror, on the wall,

Who in this land is the fairest of all?'

The mirror answered:

'You, Queen, are the fairest of all.'

And the queen was very pleased.

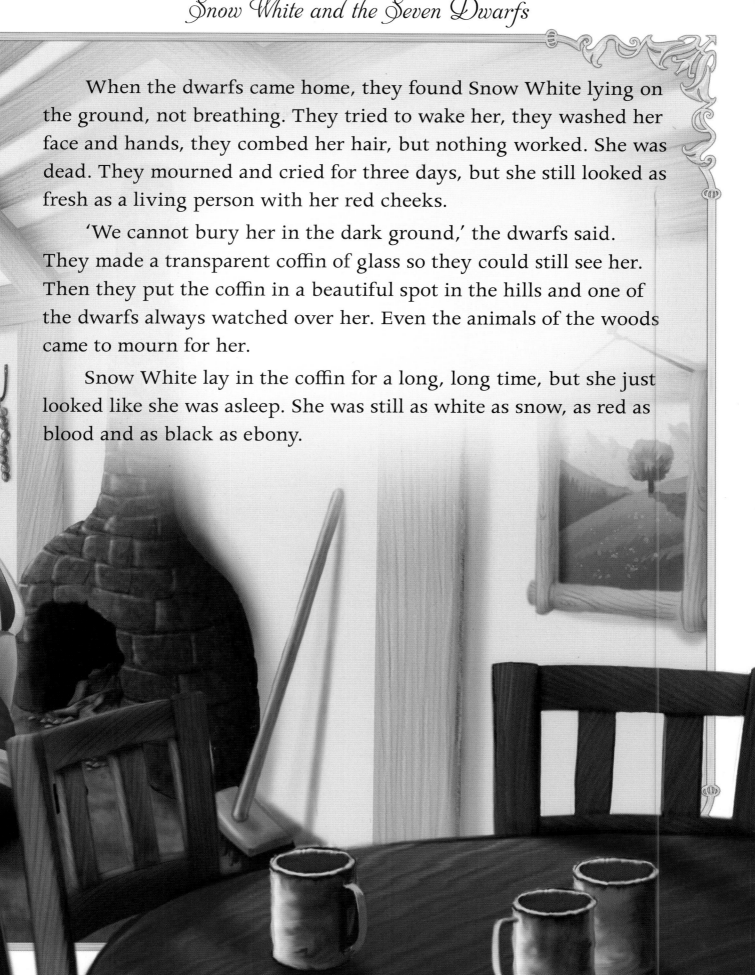

When the dwarfs came home, they found Snow White lying on the ground, not breathing. They tried to wake her, they washed her face and hands, they combed her hair, but nothing worked. She was dead. They mourned and cried for three days, but she still looked as fresh as a living person with her red cheeks.

'We cannot bury her in the dark ground,' the dwarfs said. They made a transparent coffin of glass so they could still see her. Then they put the coffin in a beautiful spot in the hills and one of the dwarfs always watched over her. Even the animals of the woods came to mourn for her.

Snow White lay in the coffin for a long, long time, but she just looked like she was asleep. She was still as white as snow, as red as blood and as black as ebony.

One day, a handsome prince entered the woods. He needed shelter for the night, and came to the dwarfs' cottage. He saw the coffin with Snow White in it. The prince immediately fell in love with Snow White, and begged the dwarfs to let him take the coffin. He offered them money, but the dwarfs said, 'We would not part with her for anything in the world.'

In despair, the prince said, 'Then please give the coffin to me. I cannot live without seeing her.'

Seeing his distress, the dwarfs took pity on him and gave him the coffin.

The moment the prince lifted the coffin to carry it home with him, the piece of poisoned apple was jolted out of Snow White's mouth and she awoke.

'Where am I?' Snow White asked.

The prince told her what had happened and said, 'I love you more than anything. Come with me to my father's castle and become my wife.'

Snow White saw the love in the prince's eyes and agreed. Their wedding was planned with great splendour.

Snow White's stepmother was invited to the prince's wedding.
After she put on her beautiful clothes, she asked the magic mirror:

'Mirror, mirror, on the wall,

Who in this land is the fairest of all?'

The mirror answered:

'You, my queen are fair, it's true,

But the young bride is a thousand times fairer than you.'

The queen was furious when she saw the bride was Snow White.
She died soon after, destroyed by her hatred and envy. Snow White
and the prince reigned happily for many years. They often visited the
dwarfs in the mountains, who had been so kind to Snow White in
her time of need.

Beauty
and the Beast

There was once a rich merchant who had three sons and three daughters. He spared no expense to give his children the best of everything. His daughters were beautiful, but the youngest was the loveliest. Everyone called her 'Beauty', which made her sisters very jealous.

The two oldest sisters were very proud and refused many offers of marriage because they were waiting for a duke or an earl to ask them. Beauty also refused several offers of marriage, saying she was too young and wished to stay with her father.

Then one day tragedy struck. The merchant's fine house burned down, with all their possessions. Then he discovered that his agents in distant countries had been cheating him out of his earnings. Finally, a great storm wiped out his fleet of ships, which were carrying the last of his goods to market. The merchant's fortune was destroyed.

All that was left was a small house in the country in the middle of a dark forest. The merchant told his children that they must move there and work for their living. The two eldest daughters thought that their fine friends in the city would take them in, but these friends forsook them in their poverty.

When they came to the house, the merchant and his sons worked the land to support them. Beauty rose at four every morning and worked, cooking, spinning and cleaning. She grew stronger and more beautiful than ever and remained cheerful for her father.

But her two sisters rose at ten and spent the day lamenting the loss of their fine clothes and friends. 'Look at our sister,' they said. 'She's such a stupid creature that she's happy with our dismal situation.'

The family had been living there for a year when the merchant received a letter. One of his ships with a rich cargo, which he had thought lost in the storm, had arrived safely to port.

The two oldest sisters were convinced that their poverty was over. They begged their father to bring back new gowns, jewels, ribbons and other trifles. The merchant begged them to be prudent, as he wasn't sure if this cargo was enough to discharge his debts, let alone set up a new fortune. Beauty alone asked for nothing. Her father, noticing her silence, asked her, 'And what shall I bring you, Beauty?'

'I only wish for your safe return, father,' she replied.

Her father was pleased but told her that she should have some pretty present and she should choose something.

'Dear father, if you insist, bring me a rose,' replied Beauty. 'I have not seen one since we arrived here and I love them so much.'

The good merchant set out to town, but when he arrived, it was as he'd feared. After a great deal of trouble, the merchant was left with little more than he had started with. He made his way home, thinking how much he wished to see his children again.

The merchant was still several hours from home as he made his way through a forest. As it grew dark, the wind howled and it started snowing heavily. The merchant realised that he was lost. He heard wolves howling and his clothes were soaked through. Suddenly, he saw a light gleaming through some trees.

As he made his way down a rough track towards the light, the merchant realised that the road was becoming easier. He came out of the forest into an avenue of trees ending at a splendid, illuminated castle.

The merchant made his way to the castle courtyard, but he was surprised to see no one about. However, he saw the stable door was open and went in, finding hay and oats laid out for his horse. The merchant went up to the castle door and entered. He walked through several splendid rooms before he found himself in a large hall with a good fire and a table set out with a feast for one person. He sat in front of the fire to warm himself and waited for the master of the house or some servants to appear, and he soon fell asleep.

The merchant woke when the clock struck eleven but still no one had come. Unable to contain his awful hunger, the merchant ate until he could eat no more. Growing braver, he made his way through more rooms until he found a chamber with a magnificent bed in it. Exhausted, he shut the door and went to sleep.

The next morning, the merchant awoke and discovered a suit of clothes laid out for him. 'Certainly, this place must belong to some fairy,' he thought, amazed.

The merchant looked out the window and saw the most beautiful gardens filled with lovely flowers, and not a trace of snow to be seen. He returned to the great hall and found breakfast laid out. 'Thank you, good fairy,' he said aloud, and then ate his breakfast.

After he had eaten, the merchant made his way outside to find the stables, but passing a rose arbour, he remembered Beauty's request. He gathered one to take to her, but then he heard an awful noise behind him. When the merchant turned around, he saw a frightful beast coming towards him and he fell to his knees.

'Ungrateful wretch!' said the Beast in a terrible voice. 'I saved your life, fed you and warmed you, and you repay me by stealing my roses, which I value above anything else in the world! You shall die for it!'

The merchant cried, 'Oh, please forgive me noble sir! I had no intention to offend. I was gathering a rose to take to my daughter, who asked me to bring her one.'

'Save your flattery!' growled the Beast. 'I am a beast, and I despise compliments!'

In despair, the merchant told the Beast of his misfortunes, why he was travelling in the forest and how Beauty had requested a rose.

The Beast listened, and then said, 'I will forgive you on one condition. You will give me one of your daughters. She must come here willingly. If one of them is brave and loves you enough, it will save your life. I will give you a month to see if any of them will return here. If not, you must come back here. And don't think you can hide, for I shall fetch you.'

The merchant reluctantly agreed. The Beast told him he must stay another night before he could leave. He did as the Beast instructed and found a meal prepared for him in the hall. The next morning, the merchant found another suit laid out for him. He breakfasted, then found his horse in the stables.

The merchant made his way home, where he was greeted by his children, who first thought his errand was a success due to his fine clothes. He handed Beauty her rose, saying to her, 'Here is your rose, although little do you know what it cost me.'

The children listened as their father told them what had happened and the two oldest daughters burst out crying. Beauty did not cry at all and the two sisters angrily accused her of causing their father's death.

'Why, our father will not suffer on my account,' replied Beauty. 'I caused the mischief, and since the Beast will accept one of his daughters, I will offer myself to him in our father's place.'

'Nay,' said the three brothers. 'We kill the monster, or perish.'

'Do not imagine you could do this,' replied their father. 'The Beast is strong. I am charmed by Beauty's offer but I will not allow it. I am old and have lived my life. I will go.'

'Then I shall follow you and take your place,' insisted Beauty. There was nothing anyone could say to persuade her otherwise

When the day arrived for her to go, she said goodbye to her brothers and sisters, but she did not cry. She and her father rode to the Beast's castle in the forest. Her father still tried to persuade her to return home but it was in vain.

When they arrived, the castle was lit up as before. In spite of her fear, Beauty could not help but admire the wonderful palace. They made their way into the great hall, where a feast for two awaited them. When they had finished eating, they heard a great roaring and then the Beast entered the hall. Beauty was terrified by his awful appearance but tried to hide it. When the Beast asked her if she had come willingly, she bravely replied, 'Yes.'

'I am pleased,' replied the Beast. Turning to the merchant, he said, 'You must leave at sunrise. Remember, you must never come here again.'

Turning to Beauty, the Beast said, 'Take your father into the next room and choose anything you wish for your father to take with him.'

Beauty and her father found two empty chests. The room was full of splendid dresses, ornaments, jewels and gold. The more they put in the chests, the more room there seemed to be, and they filled them so full that it seemed they'd need an elephant to carry them.

Beauty and her father then went to sleep and Beauty had a vivid dream. She saw a fine lady, who came to her and said, 'What you are doing will not go unrewarded. Be brave.' When Beauty awoke, she told her father the dream and it comforted him a little.

When the time came for the merchant to leave, they found two fine horses waiting in the courtyard carrying the heavy chests. Beauty did not cry until her father rode away. Then she sat in the great hall and wept, as she was sure the Beast would soon eat her.

Beauty decided to take a walk around the castle, as it was very fine. As she walked, she came to a door with 'Beauty's apartment' written above it. When she opened it, she was amazed to see how magnificent it was. She was especially delighted to see a large library, a harpsichord and some music books. 'Surely this preparation would not have been necessary if I were to be eaten,' Beauty thought to herself, and she grew less fearful.

Beauty opened a book and on the first page, she read:

Welcome Beauty, do not fear,

You are mistress of all here.

Speak your wishes, state your will,

Swift obedience meets them still.

Alas,' sighed Beauty, 'all I want is to see my poor father.'

As soon as she spoke, a great mirror on the wall showed Beauty her father being met by her brothers and sisters. Her brothers looked sorrowful but her sisters could not contain their glee at the chests of treasure. The picture faded after a moment.

That night, as Beauty was sitting down to supper, she heard the Beast approaching. She was terrified, but the Beast asked, 'Will you allow me to join you for dinner?'

'As you please,' answered Beauty. Then the Beast asked her how she had spent her time and she told him about the rooms she found. When the Beast got up to leave after they had eaten, Beauty was surprised that an hour had passed. Maybe the Beast was not as terrible as she had supposed.

As he rose, the Beast asked, 'Beauty, will you marry me?'

Beauty was terrified she would anger him by refusing, but she answered, 'No, Beast.'

The Beast sighed and turned away, saying, 'Then good night Beauty.'

Welcome Beauty, do not fear, you are mistress of all here. Speak your wishes, state your will, swift obedience meets them still.

When he had left, Beauty felt very sorry for the Beast. 'It is such a pity that someone so good natured should be so ugly.'

Beauty spent many months at the palace. Every day she found new surprises at the castle and every evening the Beast joined her for dinner and they talked for hours. Beauty got used to him and looked forward to his visits more than any other part of her day. She found the Beast was exceedingly kind and good-natured. The only worry was that every night as he left the table, the Beast asked her to marry him.

One day she said to him, 'Beast, I wish I could consent to marry you, as I see how my refusal saddens you. However, I am too sincere to make you think that might happen, but I love you as my greatest friend. Can you endeavour to be happy with that?'

'Alas, I love you with all my heart,' answered the Beast, 'but I must be happy with that, if you will promise to stay here always. Can you promise me that?'

Beauty hesitated, for that day in the mirror, she had seen her father, deathly ill from grief at her loss. 'I could promise, but I have such a desire to see my poor father that I might die if I can't,' she said.

'I would rather die myself than see you unhappy,' said the Beast. 'I will return you to your father and you will remain there and I shall die from grief.'

'No!' cried Beauty and she started to weep. 'I love you too much to be the cause of your death. Let me see my father for a month and then I shall return and stay with you forever!'

'You will be there tomorrow,' the Beast told her, 'but remember your promise. Take this ring. When it is time to return, twist it on your finger and say, "I wish to go back to my palace and see my Beast again." Sleep well Beauty and you shall soon see your father again.'

The next morning, Beauty awoke to find she was in a room in her father's house, along with a trunk filled with her clothes. She rushed to greet her father and her brothers and sisters. They were amazed to see her and asked her many questions. When they heard she was only there for a month, they lamented loudly.

As the month passed, Beauty found that nothing amused her and she found herself thinking of the palace and the Beast. When the month was over, her brothers begged her to stay a few days longer, as their father was recovering his health every day. Beauty missed the Beast, but she did not have the courage to say goodbye to her family just yet, and so, day after day, she put off her departure.

One night, she had a dream. She was wandering along a path in the palace gardens when she heard groans coming from behind some bushes. Pushing them apart, she found a cave entrance. Inside, she found the Beast stretched out on his side, dying. The fine lady from her first dream appeared and said to her, 'You are only just in time to save his life. This is what happens if people do not keep their promises!'

Beauty awoke in fright and discovered it was morning. She ran to her family and told them she must go back. That night, she said goodbye to her father and then twisted the ring on her finger, saying, 'I wish to go back to my palace and see my Beast again.' She immediately fell asleep. When she awoke the next day, she discovered she was back in her room in the palace.

Beauty put on one of her finest dresses and waited for dinner to see the Beast. But dinner time came and went and there was no sign of him. After waiting a long time, she ran through the palace trying to find him. She ran into the garden, looking for him, until she came to a path that she recognised from her dream.

Sure enough, behind some bushes was the cave, and stretched out on the ground was the Beast. Beauty ran to him and stroked his head, but he did not move or open his eyes. Crying, she ran to a fountain and fetched some water. When she sprinkled it on his head, the Beast opened his eyes.

'Oh, how you have frightened me!' she wept. 'I never knew how much I loved you until now, when I thought it was too late to tell you!'

'Can you really love something as ugly as me?' asked the Beast. 'Ah Beauty, I was dying because I thought you had forgotten me. Go to the palace and wait for me there.'

Beauty returned to the hall. The Beast came to her and sat with her to eat dinner. They talked about her visit to her family. When dinner was over, the Beast rose to leave, and then asked her, 'Beauty, will you marry me?'

'Yes, dear Beast,' she answered.

As she spoke, a blaze of light erupted outside. It seemed that fireworks were exploding outside and triumphant music was playing. Turning to the Beast to ask him what all this meant, she saw that the Beast had disappeared and in his place stood a handsome prince.

When she asked where the Beast was, the prince replied, 'You see him here. An evil witch cursed me to remain a beast until a beautiful maiden agreed to marry me without knowing who I really was. Only you were able love me for my goodness underneath my ugly form and I love you with all my heart.'

Then Beauty and the prince were transported to the prince's kingdom, where they were greeted by two stately ladies. Beauty recognised one from her dreams and the other was so grand that she must be the queen. The lady from her dreams, who was a good fairy, said, 'Queen, this is Beauty, who had the courage to rescue your son from his curse. Only your consent to their marriage is needed to make them perfectly happy.'

'I consent with all my heart!' cried the queen, and she embraced her son and Beauty. The fairy sent for Beauty's family and they joyfully arrived for the wedding, which was celebrated with the utmost splendour. Even her sisters were happy for Beauty and they all lived happily ever after.

The
Princess
and the Pea

There once lived a Prince who wished to marry a Princess. However, she had to be a real Princess.

The Prince travelled all over the world, searching for such a lady, but there was always something wrong. He found Princesses in abundance, but it seemed impossible for him to tell whether they were real Princesses. There always seemed to be something not quite right about the ladies. Finally, the Prince returned home alone to his palace, quite downcast, as he wished so much to have a real Princess for his wife.

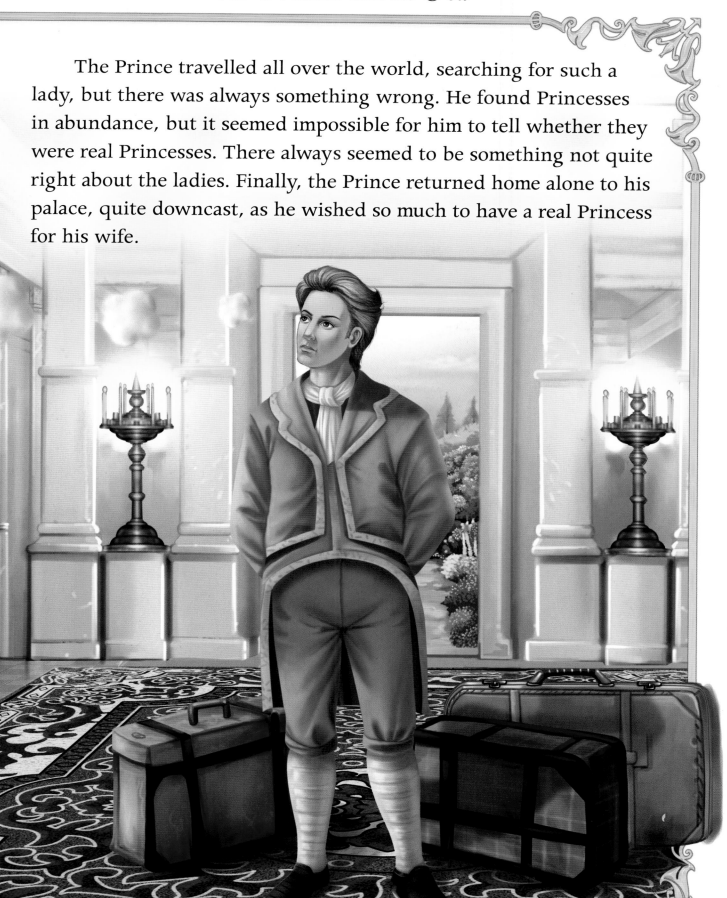

One evening, there was a terrible storm. The rain poured down in torrents, lightning cracked across the sky and thunder crashed loudly. It was pitch dark and the wind howled. Suddenly, there was a great knocking at the palace door, and the King, the Prince's father, went to open it.

When he opened the door, the King saw a Princess standing there. The rain and the wind had left her in a sad condition. Her clothes were soaked through and clung to her, and the water trickled down her hair and face. The old King showed the Princess inside and she told him that she was a real Princess.

'Indeed! We'll soon see if that's true!' thought the Prince's mother, the Queen. However, she didn't say a word to anyone about what she was planning to do. She went to the bed in the guest bedroom and rolled the bedclothes and the mattress away. The Queen laid a little pea on the bed frame and replaced the mattress and the bedclothes.

Then the Queen ordered that twenty mattresses be laid one on top of the other over the pea. Next she ordered that twenty feather eiderdowns be laid over the twenty mattresses. This was the bed where the Princess was to sleep.

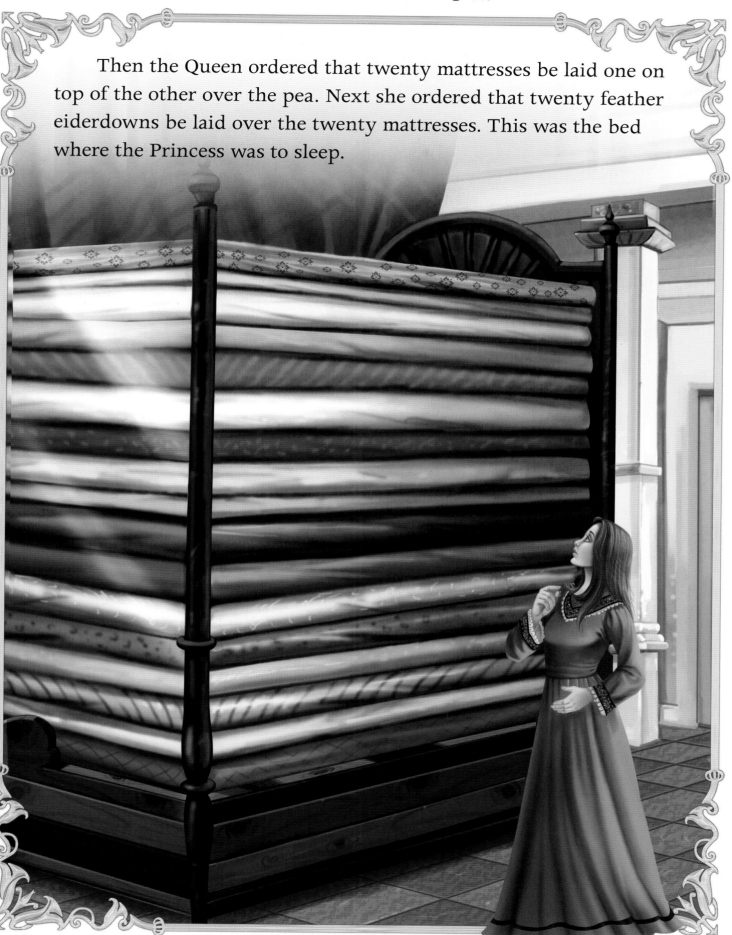

The next morning, the Queen asked the Princess how she had slept.

'Oh, very badly indeed!' exclaimed the Princess. 'I barely closed my eyes the whole night through. I do not know what was in my bed, but there was definitely something hard underneath me. I am all bruised black and blue. It has hurt me so much!'

Now the Queen knew that this Princess was, indeed, a real Princess because she had felt the pea through twenty mattresses and twenty feather eiderdowns. Only a real Princess could be so delicate and sensitive.

The Prince was overjoyed and married her, for he knew that his wife was a real Princess. As for the pea, it is said that it is kept in the castle in a cabinet of curiosities, where it can still be seen today.

The Royal Pea

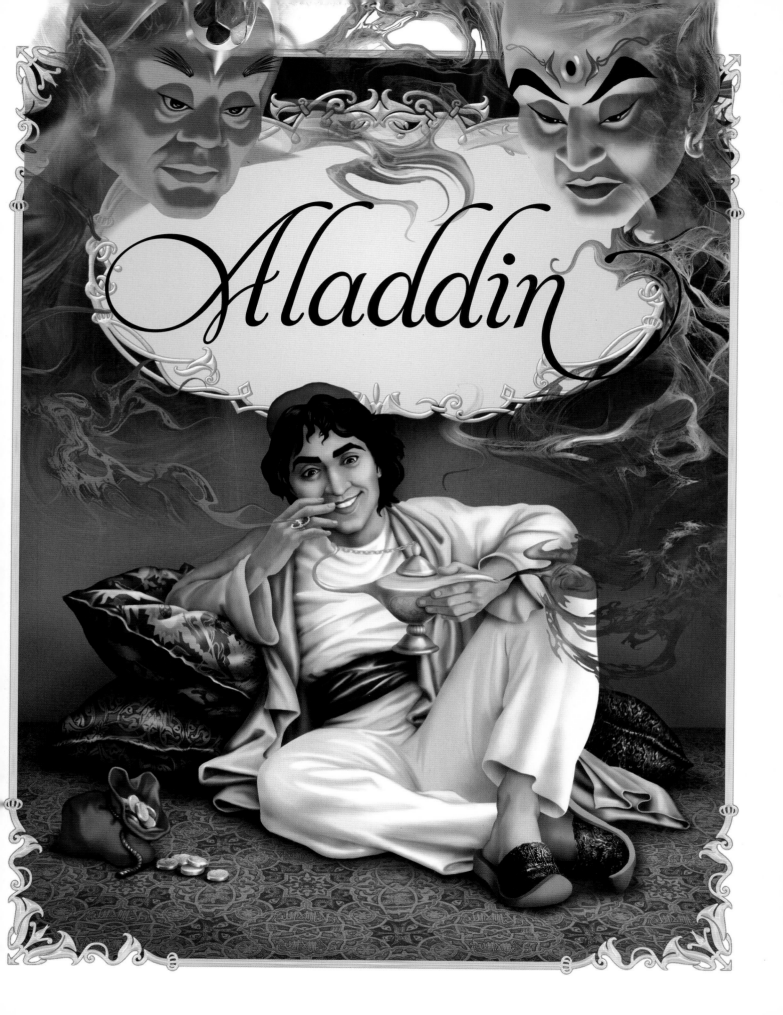

Once there lived a young man named Aladdin. His father, a tailor, had died of grief because his son was so lazy and idle. Despite this, Aladdin did not mend his ways.

One day, Aladdin was approached by a stranger, who asked him his age and if he was the son of Mustafa, the tailor. 'I am, sir,' said Aladdin, 'but my father died some years ago.'

'I thought you looked like him!' exclaimed the stranger, who was a magician. 'I am your father's brother! Tell your mother I will come and visit.'

Aladdin ran home and told his mother about his new-found uncle. 'Your father had a brother,' she said, 'but we thought he died.'

However, she prepared a meal and welcomed the magician when he arrived. 'Don't be surprised that you don't know me,' said the magician. 'I have been out of the country for forty years.'

When his uncle heard that Aladdin had no profession, he offered to stock a shop for him to make his mother proud. The next day, the magician took Aladdin out to buy some new clothes. His mother was overjoyed when she saw her son looking so fine.

The following day, the magician took Aladdin out of the city. They journeyed for a long while until they reached the mountains. At last, they came to a narrow valley. 'We will go no further,' said the magician. 'Gather some sticks and I shall make a fire.'

When it was lit, the magician threw a powder on the fire and said some magic words. The ground shook and a stone slab with a brass ring was revealed. Aladdin tried to run away in fear but the magician stopped him. 'Don't be afraid,' said the magician. 'Beneath this stone lies a treasure. It shall be yours if you do exactly as I say.'

When he heard this, Aladdin forgot his fears. Following the instructions of the magician, he grasped the brass ring and pulled, saying the names of his father and grandfather. The stone came up easily and revealed a set of steps leading down.

'Go down,' said the magician to Aladdin. 'You will find a corridor leading to three large halls. Tuck in your gown and go through them. Do not touch the walls or you will instantly die. The halls lead to a garden of fruit trees. Go through the garden until you reach a stone terrace where a lighted lamp stands. Pour out the oil in the lamp and bring it back to me.'

The magician took off a ring and gave it to Aladdin. Aladdin followed his uncle's instructions. He picked up the lamp and walked back through the garden, taking some fruit off the trees as he went. Aladdin got back to the mouth of the cave and the magician cried out, 'Be quick and give me the lamp!'

But Aladdin refused, as he wasn't safely out of the cave yet. The magician flew into a terrible rage. He threw more powder on the fire and said some magic words. The stone rolled back into place, trapping Aladdin in the cave.

The magician fled far away to another country. He was not Aladdin's uncle, but an evil magician who had read of the lamp in his books. He knew it must be retrieved by the hand of another. The magician had picked Aladdin for this very reason and planned to kill him after he got the lamp.

For two days, Aladdin remained in the dark, crying. Realising he was stuck, he clasped his hands in prayer. As he did so, Aladdin rubbed the ring, which the magician had forgotten to take from him. Suddenly, an enormous genie rose up, saying, 'I am the slave of the ring! What is your wish?'

'Save me from here!' answered Aladdin. The stone rolled back and Aladdin climbed out and struggled home.

Aladdin told his mother about the magician's trickery. He showed her the lamp and the fruits, which were actually precious stones. His mother went to cook, but she had no food or money, so Aladdin said he would sell the lamp. It was very dirty, so he rubbed it with his sleeve to clean it. Instantly, a huge genie appeared. It bowed and asked, 'What will you have?'

'Fetch us something to eat!' said Aladdin. The genie conjured up a feast on silver bowls and cups. Aladdin told his mother about the cave, the ring and the lamp. At first she begged him to sell them, but Aladdin convinced her they should use them.

After they had eaten, they sold the silverware. Aladdin and his mother were able to live like this for several years. They ate the food provided by the genie, sold the silverware and lived off the money until they needed more.

One day, the sultan ordered everyone to stay inside and close their shutters. The princess was going to the bathhouse and no one was permitted to see her face. However, Aladdin hid near the bathhouse. He caught a glimpse of the princess's face when she lifted her veil as she walked in the door. She was so beautiful that Aladdin instantly fell in love with her.

Aladdin told his mother that he meant to ask the sultan for his daughter's hand in marriage. His mother laughed but Aladdin persuaded her to go to the sultan and present his request. She took the jewels from the trees in the cave with her, wrapped in a cloth.

For six days, Aladdin's mother went to sultan's hall, waiting for an audience. Finally, the sultan said to his vizier, 'I've seen that woman in the audience chamber for six days now, carrying something in that cloth. If she's here tomorrow, see what she wants.'

The next day, Aladdin's mother was summoned to the sultan. 'Tell me what you want, good woman,' said the sultan.

Aladdin's mother hesitated, so the sultan sent everyone away except for the vizier, promising he wouldn't take offence at what she was going to say. She told him of her son's love for his daughter and unfolded the jewels and presented them to the sultan.

The sultan was amazed by the priceless jewels. He turned to the vizier and said, 'See how much this man values my daughter? Surely I should allow them to marry.'

However, the vizier wanted his son to marry the princess. He convinced the sultan to wait three months before he gave his permission. The vizier hoped that he could make a richer gift and win the princess for his son. So the sultan agreed to Aladdin's proposal but told his mother that they must wait three months.

Aladdin waited. Two months went by, and then one day he discovered the townspeople rejoicing. 'Tonight the vizier's son is to marry the sultan's daughter!' they told him.

Aladdin fetched the lamp. He rubbed it and the genie appeared before him, saying, 'What is your will?'

'The sultan has broken his promise,' replied Aladdin. 'The princess marries the vizier's son. Bring them here tonight.'

'I obey, master,' said the genie.

Under the laws of the city, a couple were not married until they spent a night together. That night, the genie transported the princess and the vizier's son to Aladdin's house. 'Take this man and put him outside.' Aladdin said to the genie, 'Bring him in at daybreak.'

The genie took the vizier's son out, leaving the princess with Aladdin. 'Do not fear,' he said to her. 'You are promised as my wife and no harm shall come to you.'

The princess spent a miserable night, as she was too frightened to sleep. In the morning, the genie fetched in the cold, shivering bridegroom and transported them back to the palace.

When the sultan came to wish them good morning, the vizier's son hid and the princess looked miserable. She wouldn't speak to her father but told her mother how she had been carried to a strange house where the vizier's son had been sent away. Her mother told her that it must have been a dream.

But the same thing happened the following night. The next morning, the princess told the sultan what had happened. The vizier's son refused to marry the princess, saying he'd rather die than go through another night like that.

Aladdin sent his mother to remind the sultan of his promise, but the sultan was reluctant to grant his permission. He told Aladdin's mother, 'Your son may marry my daughter, but he must send me forty basins of gold filled with jewels, carried by forty slaves, who are lead by another forty slaves, all splendidly dressed.'

Aladdin's mother went home, thinking all was lost. But Aladdin summoned the genie of the lamp and soon eighty slaves arrived, forty of them carrying gold basins filled with jewels. They set out for the palace with Aladdin's mother. Everyone crowded to see them.

Aladdin's mother entered the palace and bowed to the sultan. The sultan said, 'Tell your son I wait for him with open arms.'

Aladdin called the genie. 'I want a scented bath, an embroidered robe, a fine horse and twenty slaves. I need six slaves to wait on my mother and ten thousand gold pieces in ten purses.' And it was done.

Aladdin mounted his horse and rode to the palace, followed by slaves throwing gold pieces to the cheering crowd. The sultan welcomed Aladdin and asked him to marry his daughter that day, but Aladdin said he had to build a palace for the princess first.

Aladdin said to the genie, 'Build a palace of finest marble set with precious stones. Put a large domed hall in the middle with walls of gold and silver. Put windows of diamonds and rubies in each wall. There must be stables, horses, grooms and slaves.'

The palace was finished the next day. Aladdin and his mother went to the sultan's palace. They were met by musicians and dancers. The princess was charmed by the handsome Aladdin. The princess told him that she was very happy to obey her father and marry him. They danced at the wedding feast until midnight and then returned to Aladdin's palace.

The next day, Aladdin invited the sultan to see the palace. The sultan was astounded, but the jealous vizier hinted that it must be the work of magic. However, Aladdin had won the heart of the sultan, who made Aladdin the captain of his armies. Over the next few years, Aladdin lived happily with the princess and won several battles for the sultan, but he remained courteous and modest.

However, far away, the evil magician remembered Aladdin. He was furious when he heard that Aladdin had escaped, married a princess and was living in great honour and wealth instead of perishing. This could have only happened with the lamp and so the magician set out to seize it for himself. He was determined to see Aladdin ruined.

When he arrived in the town, the magician discovered that Aladdin had gone hunting. The magician went to the market and bought a dozen new lamps. He put them in a basket and dressed as a peddler. He made his way towards Aladdin's palace, crying out, 'New lamps for old!' The townspeople laughed at this poor trade.

The princess was sitting in the garden when she heard the crowd laughing. She sent a slave to find out what the fuss was about. When she heard that a peddler was exchanging old lamps for brand new ones, she told the slave to take the old lamp from the shelf and exchange it. Now this was the magic lamp, which Aladdin could not take hunting with him.

Amidst the jeers of the crowd, the slave made the exchange. The magician ran out of the city gates. He waited until night and then rubbed the lamp. At his command, the genie carried the palace, the princess and the magician far away.

The sultan was shocked that Aladdin's palace was gone. He asked the vizier what had happened and the jealous vizier said that it was magic, for which the penalty was death. The sultan sent soldiers out for Aladdin, who bound him in chains. But the people loved Aladdin and they followed them to the palace.

The sultan ordered the executioner to cut off Aladdin's head, but the crowd forced their way in to rescue him. They were so threatening that the sultan ordered the executioner to stop. Aladdin begged to know what he had done. 'Where is my daughter?' demanded the sultan. 'Find her or you will lose your head!'

Aladdin begged the sultan to give him forty days to find her. If he couldn't, he promised to return and the sultan could do what he wished. The sultan agreed and Aladdin went to find the princess.

Aladdin wandered for several days. No one could tell him what happened to his palace. He came to a river and in despair decided to throw himself in. He knelt to pray, but as he did, he rubbed the magic ring, which he still wore. The genie of the ring appeared and asked him what his wish was. 'Bring my palace back!' said Aladdin.

'I do not have that power,' answered the genie of the ring. 'Only the genie of the lamp can do that.'

'Can you take me to my palace outside my wife's window?' asked Aladdin.

Aladdin found himself far away under the princess's window. When she saw Aladdin again, the princess was delighted and kissed him joyfully. 'Tell me, my love,' asked Aladdin, 'what happened to the old lamp that I left on the shelf?'

'It is all my fault!' exclaimed the princess. She told how she had exchanged the lamp. 'The magician has it,' she said. 'He wishes to marry me and says that my father beheaded you, but I refuse him.'

Aladdin went into a nearby town, bought a powder and snuck into the palace. 'Put on a beautiful dress and pretend you have forgotten me,' he told the princess. 'Invite him to eat with you and ask to try some wine. I will tell you what to do.'

The princess dressed in her finest clothes and received the magician. 'I have decided to mourn for Aladdin no more,' she said. 'Eat with me and let us try some of the wines of your country.'

The magician was dazzled by her beauty and smiles and ran to the wine cellar. Meanwhile, the princess put some of Aladdin's powder into the magician's cup. The magician returned, drank the wine from his cup and fell down dead. Aladdin quickly retrieved the lamp and asked the genie to set things right. How pleased the sultan was to see the palace returned and his daughter safe!

Aladdin thought he could live in peace, but it wasn't to be. The magician's brother was even more wicked and cunning and came to avenge him. He stole a holy woman's clothes and went to Aladdin's palace, his face hidden by a veil. A crowd gathered around him as he went, thinking he was a holy woman, and asked for a blessing.

The princess heard the crowd and told a servant to see what was going on. The servant said it was a holy woman who could cure people with her touch. The princess invited the false holy woman to the palace. The magician's brother looked around the palace and said it was very fine. 'However,' he said, 'it is lacking something.'

'What is that?' asked the princess.

'Hang an egg of the mystical bird, the roc, from the dome and it would be the wonder of the world,' answered the false holy woman.

After this, the princess thought of nothing but a roc's egg. She told Aladdin that her joy in the palace was ruined because it didn't have a roc's egg. 'If that is all, you shall soon be happy,' he replied.

Aladdin rubbed the lamp and commanded the genie to bring him a roc's egg. But the genie gave a shriek that shook the palace.

'Haven't I done enough for you?' demanded the genie. 'Now you want the egg of the fearsome roc! This request doesn't come from you, but from the evil magician's brother! He is here, disguised as a holy woman! He has requested this, hoping you would be killed by the roc. This man intends to murder you.'

Aladdin told the princess that his head ached and he wished the holy woman to cure him. But when the false holy woman came near, Aladdin seized his dagger and slew him. The princess was horrified, but Aladdin said, 'This is no holy woman! This is the magician's evil brother!' and he told her how she had been tricked.

After this, Aladdin and the princess lived a long and happy life.
When the sultan died, Aladdin succeeded him as ruler and reigned
with the for many happy years.

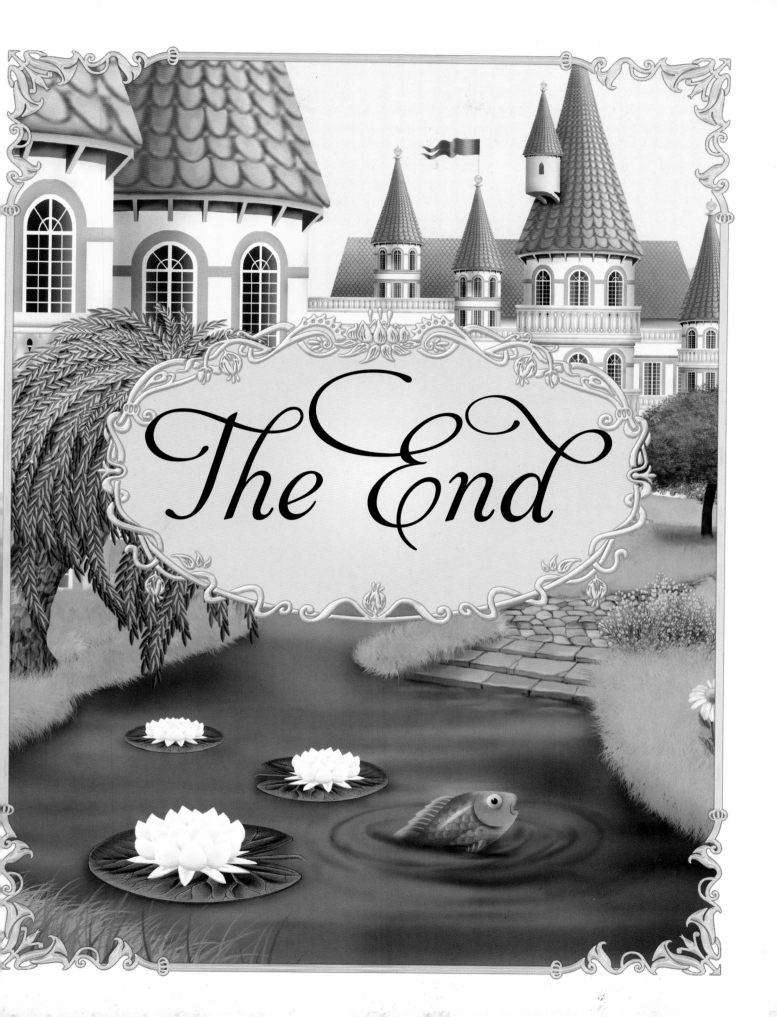

Illustrators

MELISSA WEBB

The Little Mermaid

Cinderella

Beauty and the Beast

MIRELA TUFAN

Sleeping Beauty

Aladdin

DEAN JONES

Snow White and the Seven Dwarfs

SUZIE BYRNE

The Princess and the Frog

BRIJBASI ART PRESS

Rapunzel

Thumbelina

The Princess and the Pea